THE DIAMOND K SHOWDOWN

Warned off his Cottonwood Creek spread by Spur riders, Ewan McGill is determined to sit it out. Then, one terrible day three weeks later, his house is burned down, his wife Verity is kidnapped and his ten-year-old son murdered. But worse is to come, for Marshal Lew Drummond winds up dead on the same day. Now Ewan McGill must take matters into his own hands and with mercantile owner, Jake Harding, he sets off for Jackson's Hole, burning for revenge and the release of Verity . . .

WILL KEEN

THE DIAMOND K SHOWDOWN

Complete and Unabridged

LINFORD
Leicester

First published in Great Britain in 2001 by
Robert Hale Limited
London

First Linford Edition
published 2003
by arrangement with
Robert Hale Limited
London

British Library CIP Data

Keen, Will
    The Diamond K showdown.
    —Large print ed.—
    Linford western library
    1. Western stories
    2. Large type books
    I. Title
    823.9'14 [F]

    ISBN 0–7089–4862–6

Published by
F. A. Thorpe (Publishing)
Anstey, Leicestershire

Set by Words & Graphics Ltd.
Anstey, Leicestershire
Printed and bound in Great Britain by
T. J. International Ltd., Padstow, Cornwall

This book is printed on acid-free paper

Part One

THE KILLING

1

Three of them. A couple of miles back, far beyond the reach of the high bluff's long shadow but riding steadily west. Three riders who, at that distance, were little more than ruddy shapes atop lathered mounts rimmed with fire in the blazing glory of the setting sun. The glint of weapons at belt and saddle boot. A haze of dust drifting, settling.

The distance closing even as he watched.

The sudden, brilliant flash of light on glass.

McGill rolled away from the rimrock, cursing softly, slithered down the steep rock shelf on his backside and came to his feet running like a madman. The sun was a blinding ball of fire on the horizon; at the foot of the long slope the two horses were dark silhouettes almost lost in the shade of the cottonwoods.

Johnny met him, anxiety in his big blue eyes.

'They still comin', Pa?'

'A long way back,' McGill lied, his breathing ragged, and he dropped a hand to tousle the boy's hair. 'Mount up and we'll push on. With luck we'll be in Coyote Gulch before full dark.'

Or maybe not, he thought, vivid images of the stab of bright light from the man using field-glasses nagging at him like a persistent headache. If he had spotted McGill they'd know for sure they were closing. With that knowledge, would they go for the quick kill? Or had they already decided that McGill would stop at Coyote Gulch for the night, figured they could take time to wash the trail dust out of their throats before carrying out Blake Seeger's orders?

Because, although he had no idea what this was about, or why Double Spur riders were following them, with the house they had wanted him to quit now burned to the ground, he had no

4

doubt that Seeger's was the wicked mind directing this madness.

Johnny was up on his pony, parched grey leaves rustling as he pushed through the drooping branches and wheeled out of the trees. McGill swung into the saddle, rode up behind him and felt a sudden rush of emotion that took away his breath. So like his ma! She had always kept her corn-coloured hair trimmed short, had always been proud of her boyish figure. Now their son was riding away from the only home he had ever known, unaware that his mother was dead — and McGill could not find the words to tell him because even now he did not know for certain.

With an instinctive glance back at the bluff that blocked sight of the pursuing riders, Ewan McGill followed his son on to the trail. Without conscious thought he let him canter ahead, allowing the space between them to grow. When it was done — when the distance had stretched to beyond a couple of hundred yards and Johnny glanced back and waved happily — he knew that he was doing it for the boy's safety. If they were overtaken, he would have that much longer to get away — and, by God, if it came to that, McGill would make sure the men paid with their blood for every yard they gained.

The boy knew the way. He had first ridden the trail into town when he was three years old, tow head shining gold in the morning sun as he bounced atop his first pony. Since then — eight years, almost — he'd done the trip at least once a month, sometimes riding, sometimes taking the buckboard with his ma or pa; sometimes, in the past couple of years, proudly making the trip to Coyote Gulch on his own, where Jake Harding would meet him outside his mercantile and, with a hidden smile, make out that the boy was sharing the heavy work of loading provisions.

But no longer.

McGill's jaw muscles bunched as he

angrily shook his head to clear away frustration at his own helplessness, the pain of a loss he would not yet allow himself to admit. And again, instinctively, he glanced back and saw only emptiness. Through their settling dust the west side of the sunlit bluff was a rocky escarpment fast falling away into the distance, locked in stillness, the only movement in his wake his own lengthening shadow.

Sudden decision put his spurs to the sorrel, and he rode fast until he was alongside his son. The thud of hooves was heard, the flash of a bright grin was his greeting, his approach suddenly part of a familiar game. Johnny McGill kicked his pony into a gallop, pulled away fast, glanced back to shoot at his pa with a pointed forefinger, then in deadly earnest settled down to the race.

They entered Coyote Gulch's main street in that fashion, man and boy riding neck and neck into the shadowy canyon of false fronts but with Ewan McGill carefully letting his son's pony win by a nose. Their arrival was duly noted, but with the lack of surprise that was to be expected of a habitual occurrence. An appreciative whistle from old Mose, the swamper, standing outside the saloon, drew a grin of triumph from the boy. And a block beyond Soaper's Livery, Jake Harding looked up and waited expectantly on the gallery of the mercantile.

But Ewan McGill wasn't going that way. With his face once again carefully wooden as he fought to hide the worry eating away at his heart, he called quietly to his son, watched him wheel across the street towards the store, then swung in to draw rein outside the marshal's office.

★ ★ ★

The room was alive with dust motes dancing in shafts of sunlight. An iron stove stood chill in a corner and an open roll-top desk was littered enough to spill papers like Fall leaves on to the dirt floor. On the back wall a gun rack was bright with rifles and shotguns kept oiled for action. On other walls, framed certificates, curling Wanted dodgers and newspaper cuttings were yellowing with age.

'I guess your boy beat you again,' Ed Thorpe said laconically. He was sitting back in a swivel chair, his boots threatening to edge more papers from the surface of the desk as he idly whittled at a stubby mesquite twig.

McGill looked absently at the deputy, turned his head to let his gaze drift to the inner door as he tipped his Stetson back with a forefinger.

'Lew out back?'

'Rode out at dawn. Darcy Griffin's been losin' too many horses.'

McGill shook his head, eased himself gingerly on to a rickety chair. 'Lookin' into something like that, Lew could be gone most of the day.'

Thorpe shrugged. 'Trouble?'

A match flared as he put down knife and stick and lit a cigarette. He shifted his boots on the scarred desk, crossed his ankles, his eyes watchful through the smoke.

'About the time Lew was leaving town,' McGill said, 'three Spur men were havin' fun burnin' down my house.'

The shrewd eyes narrowed. Muscle bunched in the deputy's lean jaw. 'The hell they did! Spur? Why in God's name would they do that?'

'I was warned, three weeks ago. Told to move out, or face the consequences.'

Thorpe shook his head. 'Don't make sense. Christ, you're thirty miles west of Seeger's spread, your cows wallow in a muddy creek, his graze on the banks of the Brazos.' He shook his head in disbelief. 'How long you been there now, McGill?'

'Nine, ten years.'

'And in that time Blake's been a good friend?'

'We've mostly seen eye to eye.'

'With good reason. To a spread the size of Spur, you've never been a threat,

10

never will be.' The deputy drew on his cigarette, trickled smoke, thought for a few moments, then looked hard at McGill. 'What about your wife? You say your place went up in smoke, yet you and the boy're here in town, rode in like nothing happened.'

'For his sake.' McGill met the deputy's eyes, saw the impersonal look of a lawman who knew him only as a small rancher who picked up supplies from time to time, and had been known to drop in for the occasional evening playing cards in the saloon with Jake Harding and his friends. McGill knew that compared to Blake Seeger he was a small fish in a very big pool, and he was sitting in the deputy's office telling a tale that questioned the big rancher's morals.

'Maybe I'd better save the story for Lew.'

'You still ain't answered my question.'

McGill took a breath. 'Me and the boy were ridin' out in the hills. By the

11

time we got back, all that was left of the house was a pile of hot ash between the barns and the corral, the big stone chimney pokin' up at the sky.' He could feel the pain behind his eyes, and shook his head irritably. 'There was no sign of Verity.'

A thick silence hung still in the office. Thorpe sucked his teeth, kicked his legs off the desk and stood up.

'Could've been strangers.'

'They were riding Spur horses.'

The deputy frowned. 'You saw them?'

'Last time.' McGill nodded slowly, remembering, his lips pursed. 'Three weeks back, for sure. I told you, I was warned.'

'Right.' Thorpe nodded, his manner easing. 'So the fellers done this, they could be mavericks, no connection with Spur.'

'Three weeks ago they were close enough for me to read their brands. Today . . . '

'Today they weren't.' Bluntly, this,

and McGill shook his head irritably.

'I saw three men. Not close. But they were built the same, dressed the same, and if they were ridin' Spur horses then — '

'Jesus, McGill, this is like pullin' teeth. When did you see them?'

McGill forced a thin smile. 'Last time was no more than a quarter hour ago, when me and my boy were managin' to stay far enough ahead of them so they couldn't use their pistols. I think one was usin' glasses, so they'll know where we were headin'.' He shrugged. 'Let's say I expect to see them again pretty soon — only this time I'm ready.'

Thorpe's face was wooden.

'Not in Coyote Gulch, you're not.'

'Whatever happens won't be of my doing. But an hour ago I left the burnt ruins of my house, was tracked into town by three men — the same three men who warned me this would happen.'

'So keep your head down. Where's your boy now?'

'Where he always is when he hits town.'

'Harding's?'

McGill nodded, scarcely listening, his head half turned towards the street window.

Watching him, Thorpe said quietly, 'Ain't nobody ridden in. I've had my eyes and ears open, and all that's told me is you could've made a mistake.'

'Here,' McGill said angrily, rising from the chair and thrusting his arm across the desk. 'The stink of smoke's on my clothes, for all I know the stink of charred flesh — '

'Easy, now,' Thorpe said. He came around the desk, touched McGill's shoulder. 'Why don't you go join your boy over at the store? If what you say's right, he needs lookin' after. About this time I usually take a walk around town. If any of Seeger's boys have rode in . . . '

The deputy's words trailed off, unfinished, and as he was expertly shepherded towards the door McGill

14

knew that there was nothing more he could do, or say.

He stepped out into evening shadows washed by the yellow light of oil lamps, quickly crossed the street and stamped up on to the gallery of Jake Harding's store. As he opened the door he was greeted by a waft of warm familiar odours that reminded him of his kitchen at home, and when realization hit him he was moved almost to tears.

Then, from out back, the high-pitched laughter of young boys snapped him back to reality. Clearing his throat, he walked around heavy grain sacks and tall rails of frocks and island counters stacked with a thousand and one items intended to meet the daily needs of working families, almost cracked his head on a hanging lantern, and saw Jake Harding look up from the desk where he was doing some figuring in a big leather-backed ledger.

'He's ate,' the grizzled storekeeper said, swiftly weighing up McGill with an eagle-eyed glance. 'Got his energy back; him and my boy doin' things so there ain't no room for bad thought.'

'Best thing,' Ewan McGill said huskily. He shook Harding's meaty hand, then wandered over to the pot-bellied stove while the storekeeper put away his pens and closed the ledger with a bang.

'So,' Harding growled, joining McGill in the warm corner of the big, comfortable store and taking out his blackened corn-cob pipe, 'what the hell's been going on out there on Cottonwood Creek?'

McGill reached for a straight-backed chair used mostly by the ladies of Coyote Gulch when waiting to be served, straddled it and with his elbows resting on the back began fashioning a cigarette.

'How much did Johnny tell you?'

'Told me your house was burned down.' Harding was leaning back against a counter stacked with tins, ankles crossed, smoke from his pipe swirling like river mist. 'Never mentioned Verity.'

Feeling the stiffness of his own face, aware of Harding's patient stare, McGill struck a match on the stove, trickled his share of fresh smoke into the atmosphere and watched it drift in the lamplight.

'That's because he knows nothing. Nor do I.'

'There may not be much to tell,' Harding said, 'but I'd be interested in hearing what you've got.'

'We rode out soon after dawn, spent the day up in the hills east of the Brazos. Johnny got himself a couple of jack-rabbits with my old Winchester. We reached home before sunset.' McGill stopped, listened to the sudden silence out back, looked helplessly at the big storekeeper.

Harding sighed. 'I guess this hurts some.'

'Some.' McGill took a breath, shrugged. 'It looked like the house had been burning for most of the day. I . . . '

He hesitated, stared at the glowing end of the cigarette, said, 'The barns were untouched. I couldn't see the buckboard, so I thought maybe Verity had headed for town. But . . . '

'But?'

'It was on the trail, a mile away from the spread. Just the wagon. No horse, no damage, no . . . no bloodstains.' He cleared his throat, shook his head. 'But there was plenty of horse sign, on the trail and all around the wagon; then heading off into the woods to the north.'

Jake Harding cursed softly. 'Even a boy Johnny's age can draw conclusions.'

'Or jump to them, end up holdin' the wrong end of the stick.'

'He knows his home has gone, he sees something like that he'll have a fair idea his ma went with it — whoa, now!' Harding held up a hand as McGill started up out of the chair, watched him settle back, spread both hands placatingly. 'That was said without thought, Ewan, and I apologize. There

18

ain't a one of us here knows what went on. All we can figure is, Verity took off in that buckboard, but after that . . . '

'After that, you're probably right in one respect: she didn't go with the house, but she's dead.'

'For God's sake, Ewan, you don't know that.'

'But if she is — '

'If she is, you've still got your boy and — '

He came forcefully away from the counter, the corncob clamped in a big fist.

'Goddamn, why the hell are we talking this way?' Angrily, he ran his fingers through his iron-grey hair, paced across the board floor, back again. 'You tell Lew Drummond any of this?'

'Lew's out of town.'

'Yeah. Chasin' horse-thieves.' He nodded speculatively. 'What about Thorpe?'

'He knows enough.'

'Which is how much?'

19

'I told him we were followed into town. He's doin' his rounds, keepin' his eyes — '

He broke off as the door to the back opened and Min Harding poked her grey head through.

'Jake, did you tell Zeb he could go out?'

Harding frowned. 'At this time of night?'

'I guess that's a no — but he's gone anyway.' She saw McGill and smiled. 'Johnny's with him, Ewan. Nothing to worry about, but it is getting late and — '

Somewhere, out in the street, a shot cracked out, then another. There was a thin, quavering cry of anguish, abruptly strangled.

Min Harding gasped, and clapped a hand to her mouth.

With a sick dread in his heart, McGill ran for the door.

2

Ewan McGill hit the mercantile's broad gallery already slapping leather, leaped on to the plankwalk with the dull metal of his pistol catching the faint light. After the comparative brightness of the store the street was an ill-lit, shadowy canyon in which danger lurked. Lamplight flickered as dark figures passed uncurtained windows to creep along the plankwalks. Someone called out, an uneasy question that went unanswered. The air reeked of gunsmoke.

A swift glance to left and right told McGill that the open street was deserted. Cautiously, he stepped down into the dust. At once, clearly visible as the cold light of the rising moon slanted down across the false fronts, he saw the small, crumpled figure lying alongside the trough in front of Stolt's Livery.

'Johnny,' he whispered hoarsely.

Behind him, Jake Harding's boots thudded as he came out of the shop.

'Zeb's jest walked in,' he called. 'They were playin' hide and go seek, he reckons Johnny slipped away in the dark — '

But McGill wasn't listening. The shock of seeing his son lying in the dust had set his nerves singing like taut wires, his mind racing. He guessed that the men who had gunned down a defenceless kid had done so to draw him out. They'd followed him into town blind, likely set about hunting him down. Johnny, playing an innocent game, had been caught cold.

So where were they?

At his shoulder, Harding said softly, 'Careful, boy. There's horses tied outside the saloon, they'll be watchin' you from the shadows.'

'Yeah, I'm pinned down by men I can't see, with my son lyin' in the street.'

'Better that — for a few minutes

longer — than seein' his pa die tryin' to reach him.'

'If he's bleeding his life away, he ain't got a few minutes.'

'Goddamn!' Harding swore. 'Where the hell's Ed Thorpe?'

'Christ knows — but I can't wait.'

'Ewan, for God's sake!'

Harding's big hand grabbed for a shoulder, slipped off as McGill spun away and leaped up on to the plankwalk. Ignoring the storekeeper's whispered warnings he ducked into the shadows, heart thundering as he flattened against the wall and waited with narrowed eyes for the crack of the shot, the killing impact of hot lead.

No, it's too far, he thought, as the silence dragged on. They were waiting until he got close, until he loomed large and they had a certain kill — and because with a pistol that was mighty close, he had breathing space, room to manoeuvre.

He took a breath, began edging along the wall towards the end of the block beyond which lay old man Stolt's livery barn. His eyes flicked back and forth between the crumpled figure lying in the dust, to the shadows on the opposite side of the street — because it was from there, surely, that the attack would come.

A movement to his right, a woman's worried cry, stopped him dead, prickled the hairs on his neck and jerked his head around. McGill let his breath go. Light was flooding from the store's open doorway. Jake Harding's stovepipe boots were kicking up dust as he pounded across the street. He was carrying a shotgun. As McGill watched, he reached the far plankwalk, and his bulk was lost in the shadows.

McGill reached up, dashed the cold sweat from his brow. Again, he edged along the wall, pistol held high. His eyes resumed their watchfulness.

Johnny hadn't moved.

There was no sign of Deputy Ed Thorpe.

And now McGill had reached the

end of the block.

That close to the livery, he could smell the horses. The silence was so intense his ears caught the sound of their restless movements in the dry straw, their snorts of unease. For an instant, he wished he had their ears, the sixth sense that told them something was wrong, and where lay the danger.

He looked across the open space to the crumpled figure of his son lying on his back with both arms outflung in the shadow of the horse trough, above him the flat glint of cold water. The sign of The Cross, McGill thought. He was thirty feet away, and there was no cover.

But if they wanted him it was still a tricky shot for a six-gun.

Then, whatever the risks, the blood-pull proved too great. McGill stepped down off the plankwalk, took two steps away from the buildings and was at once bathed in moonlight.

★ ★ ★

He awoke to faint snapping sounds he couldn't identify.

'Jesus Christ, my head!'

Deputy Ed Thorpe groaned the words, rolled over, shuddered as he found his face pressed into sour-smelling sawdust. He spat, levered himself up to hands and knees, head lolling painfully between bony shoulders. When he braced himself and raised it, dispersed the cobwebs with a shake of his head that he felt clear down to his boots, and peered through blurred eyes, he was looking into the black muzzle of a six-gun.

'Far enough,' the gunman said.

A shaft of pain like fierce summer lightning dragged another groan from between Thorpe's clenched teeth. He got his heels under him, teetered, then sagged backwards to finish up on his haunches with his back hard up against the boards fronting the bar.

'What happened?'

'You walked into trouble, tried to cool it, and a slug creased your skull.'

This was a big, bearded man wearing a plaid mackinaw, a battered felt hat and black pants held up by a belt with a huge silver buckle and tucked into knee-high boots. He strolled across from a table, dropped to one knee alongside the lawman.

'Leave him be — '

'Yeah, you can shove it, pal,' the bearded man said.

Big fingers gently probed the sticky wound. Thorpe winced, felt the stiffness of drying blood on his face and neck, screwed his eyes shut. When he opened them, the big man was grinning, teeth flashing white in his dark-bearded face.

'You'll live to fight another day.'

'Fight?' Thorpe's tone was bitter.

'You did what you could, in the circumstances.'

His vision clearing, Thorpe lifted an unsteady hand to move the big man to one side. Further along the plank bar, two rough men in range clothing were studiously avoiding his eyes. The worn

27

holsters at their hips were empty. Behind the bar, eyes blank, the saloonist was polishing a glass with a dirty cloth while his jaws worked on a plug of tobacco. Another man, elegantly dressed, sat at a table in the corner playing a deliberate game of solitaire — it was the snap of the new cards on the table that had knifed through Thorpe's consciousness.

'Picked early evening,' Thorpe said, eyes narrowed as he painfully gathered his thoughts. 'Place is damn near empty at this time, got it all to yourselves.'

This to the tall, lean man holding the pistol, who grinned wolfishly.

'Pure chance, friend.'

'You trailed Ewan McGill into town?'

'Did we?'

'More than that,' said the bearded man, still down on one knee alongside Thorpe. 'Feller out in the street with a Spencer, he gunned down McGill's kid.'

Thorpe swore softly, tried to push himself away from the boards. The bearded man pushed him back force-fully. His face was close to Thorpe's. Out of sight of the gunman, one bright blue eye winked. And, as the big man's hand fell away, Thorpe felt a sudden lightness at his right hip.

Beyond the lean man holding the pistol, another, stockier, man was standing with his back to the swing doors. He was half turned, a cocked shotgun covering the room. A pile of assorted weapons lay at his feet. His attention was divided. And, as every-thing began to make sense, Thorpe knew he was waiting for the sound of a shot.

'Plugged the kid to draw his pa out,' he said, thinking out loud, and recalled telling McGill to go join his boy at Harding's store. 'But maybe he's smarter than you think.'

'Actin' that way,' the man at the doors acknowledged. 'Movin' through the shadows like an Injun. But the closer he gets to his boy . . . '

Thorpe grunted. Aware that the big

man, under cover of his wide body and the loose mackinaw, was easing back the hammer of the pistol, he said loudly, 'Where is the kid?'

'He was plugged in the street, dropped by the livery,' said the lean gunslinger. 'Looks kinda forlorn, out there in the moonlight,' he said, and his grin was cruel. 'Like my pard said, the closer McGill gets the harder it'll be to — '

'Blade!'

'Yeah?'

The man with the shotgun had rested the butt on his hip, poked his head outside the saloon. Now he stepped back inside, said softly, 'Feller from the store came across the street. Looked like he was totin' a shotgun.'

'He comes too close, blow him in half.'

'What about McGill?'

'Skinner's about to take him,' said the man called Blade, and his chuckle was a cruel sound. 'How long does it take a man to walk a block in Coyote

Gulch? Right now he must be close enough to look into his kid's sightless eyes, and that makes the rest a duck shoot.'

And even as he spoke, the evening's stillness was split asunder by the crack of a single shot.

★　★　★

When the attack came, he moved like a startled jack-rabbit and without conscious thought.

The action saved his life.

He had walked ten long paces across moonlit, open space. When his boots squelched in wet mud and he took the final step to his son, he knew he was too late. Johnny was on his back in the dirt. The cold water dripping from a thin split in the wooden horse trough had splashed on to his upturned face, pooled in the hollows formed by his eye sockets. But he had felt nothing. The blood from his wound soaked the front of his shirt, and the eyes that stared wetly up at the rising moon saw nothing of its pure brightness.

McGill dropped to his knees, gunman forgotten, his throat clogged tight with grief and a swelling anger — and the bullet from the rifle that cracked wickedly across the street passed over his head with a sinister whine.

Instinctively, he threw himself sideways and rolled. The movement carried him across the warm, sticky limpness of Johnny's body. His head cracked sickeningly against cold timber. Icy water trickled down his neck.

The second shot holed the trough and water gushed, a glittering stream in the moonlight. Disorientated, his mind numb, McGill leaned out to snap two fast wild shots at the far plankwalk, ducked back as the rifle cracked, caught the flicker of movement and the pound of boots as Jake Harding came running.

The sudden deadly danger bearing down on him from along the plankwalk spooked the gunman.

'Jeffers, Blade, get out here!' he roared.

As his words rang out, he stepped out of the shadows. He was black garbed, black of hair. Teeth gleamed white as his lips drew back in a snarl. The rifle he had used to murder Johnny McGill dangled in his left hand. He made a fast draw with his right and opened up on the advancing storekeeper with his six-gun. Slugs thunked into timber. Splinters hissed from a shop front. A window shattered, and at the tie rail, horses began backing and tossing their heads, eyes rolling. Then Harding's shotgun flashed and roared as he let go with one barrel. Lead shot buzzed like a swarm of angry hornets. The gunman hurriedly flattened against the wall.

Ears ringing to the roar of gunfire, McGill uncoiled, and exploded from the trough's cover.

He sped across the street at a crouching run, six-gun blazing. As he did so, the saloon's swing doors were driven open by a kick. A stocky man leaped out, shotgun swinging high. He flashed a glance down the plankwalk. Then McGill's swift approach in the brightening moonlight caught his eye, and he hesitated. He swung around to face the street. In the gloom of the deep shadows tight up against the saloon his eyes glistened white and wild.

McGill triggered a desperate shot, saw the man's shirt sleeve billow, heard his roar of pain. Then the six-gun's hammer clicked on an empty chamber. As the stocky man stumbled towards the edge of the plankwalk, blood blossomed dark on his arm. But his right hand was lifting the shotgun. The twin muzzles were like evil black eyes, hunting McGill. He veered, ducked between the flashing hooves of the milling horses and under the tie-rail, heard the rattle of gunfire from the saloon, the sound of Ed Thorpe's voice raised in fury. Then the shotgun roared.

It was as if McGill's thigh had been clawed by a cougar. Pain burned into his groin like streaks of liquid fire. His leg buckled. He went down, outstretched hand grabbing futilely at the cold night air, hit the dirt with a thump and heard the roar of the shotgun as Harding let go with the second barrel. And he was rolling, teeth bared with pain and both hands clamped to his leg, when the stocky gunman toppled lifelessly off the sidewalk and fell between the snorting horses to land on him like a wet grain sack and drive the breath from his body.

Hands red with blood, McGill stiff-armed the dead weight off his chest, sucked in a mouthful of air and grabbed for the tie-rail's upright. When he climbed to his feet, Jake Harding was alongside him, down off the plankwalk with thick legs braced as he fumbled in his vest pocket for fresh shotgun shells. His eyes were everywhere, his jaw tight.

'Watch yourself, feller, there's two more — '

'Give me your pistol.'

Without pause, Harding drew his Colt, tossed it to McGill, said, 'For Christ's sake stay behind the horses.'

A rapid tattoo of shots drilled through his terse warning. Again the saloon doors were kicked open, and a man came tumbling out, a six-gun in each fist. He was tall and gangling. His glistening face was split by a savage grin, and he was snapping shots blind into the saloon while his slitted eyes rapidly searched the street. His swift glance alighted on Harding. He stepped back against the wall alongside the door. His first hurried shot whined over Harding's head. The second clipped the shotgun as the storekeeper brought it level, tore it from his hands.

Then McGill was shooting.

He fired twice, saw a shot punch into the wall alongside the tall gunslinger, the second shatter the saloon window. Then the black-garbed gunman stepped coolly out of the shadows. He snapped a shot at McGill, watched him duck back into a crouch, then swivelled so that he and the lean man stood back to back. With one man facing the saloon, the other the street, they moved awkwardly towards the horses.

For the third time the saloon's swing doors crashed open. A massive, bearded man leaped out like a longhorn exploding from thick scrub, side-stepped to make way for Ed Thorpe.

'That's it!' Thorpe roared. 'It's finished, all over, throw down your guns!'

Pistol held cocked, McGill eased himself upright. Harding was down on one knee, groping for his shot-gun. He found it, came up and shot a calculating glance at Thorpe and the bearded man, flanking the doorway. For several tense, strained seconds, the town of Coyote Gulch waited while the choice offered to the Spur riders of a sensible climb-down or a bloody gunfight balanced on a shaky fence.

Then the black-garbed gunman spat a vicious curse. With a high overarm swing he sent the useless Spencer spinning end over end towards Harding. The storekeeper jerked his grizzled head out of the way and flung up an arm. Bone cracked as the rifle hit his wrist. He was still off balance when the gunman came across the plankwalk in a flying leap that carried him on to the back of a sleek, nervous horse. A quick flick of a gloved hand released the tied reins. A continuation of the same movement jerked the horse's head around and it squealed and spun, its muscular shoulder slamming into McGill. His cocked pistol went off, the slug whining uselessly towards the night sky.

Then the gunman was past, spurs raking the horse's flanks as he sent it bounding away from the rail and out and around to race up the moonlit street.

On the plankwalk, his lean sidekick was alone and outnumbered. But in a gun battle, fortunes fluctuate, nothing has permanence.

'Skinner!' he roared.

His voice was a cry of outrage, his blazing eyes defiant. Ten feet away from him, Ed Thorpe growled a word at the bearded man, stepped back from the saloon and half turned to snap shots at the rider fast putting the dust of Coyote Gulch behind his mount's flashing hooves. The big bearded man's eyes were cool, fixed on the lean man, his pistol levelled. Down among the remaining horses, Harding was on one knee with a hand clamped to his cracked wrist, the empty shotgun forgotten in the dust.

McGill had Harding's pistol. The bearded man needed backup. As the black-garbed gunman tore up the street and the deputy's pistol roared, McGill stepped away from the horses so that the bearded man could see him, saw his swift movement caught and noted as, for a split second, the cool blue eyes shifted from the gunslinger to the street.

In that moment when concentration

lapsed and McGill, too late, cursed his foolish action, the lean gunslinger pounced.

A raking stride took him close to the man with the beard. A chopping left hand drove the levelled pistol aside. His own pistol came around in a looping blow that slashed across the big man's cheekbone and sent bright blood spurting.

McGill sprang forward, pistol raised, but the two men were locked together making a clean shot impossible. He bobbed left and right, feeling the weakness in his bloody thigh, cursing as the two men swayed. Then he became aware that the thunder of hoofbeats had faded and, with the mounted gunman gone, Ed Thorpe was spinning to face the action. But the bearded man was stunned and blinded, already going down as consciousness left him and his legs began to buckle. The lean gunman's powerful shove sent him reeling. His head cracked against Thorpe's jaw, his shoulder drove into the deputy's guts. Both men toppled backwards, splintering the plankwalk's rail. Arms flailing, the deputy landed in the dust with a thud and twisted away from the helpless big man.

Now McGill's way was clear.

As the lean gunman wheeled from the splintered rail and cut across the plankwalk towards the horses, he at last managed a shot. He saw it clip the gunman's hat, saw black eyes glint in the half-light as they picked him out, hopped awkwardly sideways as the answering shot winged his way — and stumbled over the dead gunman.

He managed to save himself from falling with a spread hand flattened in the dust, fired a second shot from an unbalanced position with his knee on the dead man's chest and knew he'd missed. And the lean gunman was moving fast, thinking even faster. Already he was in the saddle and swinging away from the saloon. He dug in his heels, flattened himself along his mount's neck as Thorpe came up on his knees and fanned the hammer of his pistol. A hail of slugs screamed after the gunman. Magically unscathed, he spurred directly across the street and, as Thorpe's hammer clicked on an empty chamber, he sent his excited mount leaping across the inert body of young Johnny McGill and disappeared down the narrow alley alongside Stolt's Livery.

In the sudden, aching silence, the big bearded man rolled over and groaned. Thorpe was on his feet, his furious eyes fixed on the mouth of the alley as he reloaded his six-gun. Ewan McGill felt numb. He pushed himself away from the dead gunman, stood shakily looking across to where Jake Harding was nursing his arm, saw the storekeeper's swift glance to where Johnny lay in the shadow of the horse trough.

Then a sleek, dark man holding a squared deck of cards emerged from the saloon and addressed the quietly fuming deputy.

'If that's not enough trouble for one night,' he said quietly, 'there's a rider coming — and he don't look too healthy.'

3

Clete Skinner was down off his horse enjoying a smoke alongside the McGills' abandoned buckboard when Blade Devlin rattled up the trail and flung himself from the saddle.

'Jesus, was that a mess!' the lean man swore as he dragged off his Stetson and slapped it angrily against his leg. His face glistened with sweat as he tossed the hat on the buckboard, bent to loosen the saddle cinch, and watched his horse wander away to join Skinner's.

'Cost me a good Spencer,' Skinner said, 'and put out Jeffers' lights.'

'And did no damn good.'

'Oh, I wouldn't say that. The kid now, he's one McGill ain't never goin' to inherit no big ranch.'

'But his pa's alive and on the loose, and him and that deputy got a good

44

look at both of us.'

Skinner trickled smoke, watched it drift away to mingle with the night mist, said softly, 'I guess they looked at them brands, too — and you know what good that'll do 'em.'

Devlin's laugh was harsh. 'Yeah. Stretch got that right. They raise a posse there's only one place they'll head, and by the time they're through talkin' to Blake Seeger — '

'We'll be long gone,' Skinner finished for him.

Devlin dragged out the makings, fashioned a cigarette. The match flared, for an instant dimming the bright, cold moonlight. When it winked out he reached for his hat and slapped it on, putting his face in deep shadow.

'Still and all,' he said uneasily, 'you know it ain't finished.'

'Nope, not while Ewan McGill's alive it ain't,' Skinner acknowledged.

'The girl neither,' Devlin said.

Skinner nodded. 'There's time,' he said easily.

'Stretch's pretty damn set on keepin' that woman alive.'

'A man don't always get what he wants.'

'He wants a ranch,' Devlin said.

'Ah!' Clete Skinner said softly. 'And in that he ain't alone; right, partner?'

Blade Devlin chuckled. 'We'll do what it takes, I guess. For us.'

'Damn right we will!' said Skinner.

4

The cold wind of death blew through the West Texas town of Coyote Gulch that night and mercilessly swept away an innocent young boy, a man called Jeffers who along with his faster sidekicks had been intent on murder, and a lawman who had ridden out to investigate a minor case of horse thieving and come back belly-down over his weary, lathered horse.

Ewan McGill saw little of Marshal Lew Drummond's return to Coyote Gulch. While Ed Thorpe and the dapper gambler helped the bearded man back into the saloon then rushed into the street to halt the horse with its gory load, he and Jake Harding moved with heavy legs and hearts as they gently lifted young Johnny McGill from the wet dirt in the lee of the horse trough.

McGill carried his dead son to Harper Wills' place, going not to the busy blacksmith's workshop that lay open to the rear alley but to that section fronting the main street where, in a room kept deliberately bare, Wills stored coffins hewn from rough timber behind a simple sign naming a second trade that required a sight more dignity and a somewhat quieter approach.

In the meantime, Harding hurried in the opposite direction to return swiftly with a shirt-sleeved, bag-toting Doc Lynch who, with a grim face, told them what was already obvious: Johnny McGill, at ten years and nine months, was dead from a single gunshot wound.

When Ewan McGill left the undertaker's, his life was empty, his grieved mind balking at what was still to come.

At his shoulder on the edge of the street, Jake Harding said, 'Come home with me?'

'Thanks, but no.'

'That leg needs lookin' at.'

'It'll keep.'

'Ewan, they'll bury him in the morning. There's nothing you can do.'

'I can't rest till I find Verity.'

Harding sighed heavily. Favouring his right wrist, he dug into his pocket for his corncob, his eyes wandering to the yellow lamplight washing out of the saloon. 'That was Lew came in. Belly down over his horse. Ed and that big feller took him into the saloon.'

'So now it's Ed's responsibility to go with me, sort this mess out.'

'Which mess?' Harding cocked his head. 'There's two killings, but no link. Drummond was after horse-thieves.'

'Maybe.'

'All right, so go where?'

'Blake Seeger's.'

A match flared. Harding's cheeks hollowed as he lit the pipe. He blew smoke thoughtfully into the evening air, squinted sideways at McGill. 'He uses a brand right, a man can tell a misleading tale.'

'I saw them twice,' McGill said wearily. 'Three weeks back. Now today.'

'Most Spur riders come into town regular . . . '

'Meaning you know them all?'

'Hell, no!' Harding said feelingly, and spat. 'No, I don't. And in any case, Seeger'll have been hirin' for the round-ups. But this . . . ' He shook his head. 'Why in hell would a man of Blake Seeger's standing hound you, have your boy killed?'

'That's what I intend to find out,' McGill said.

He swung away from Harding and limped across the street. As he stepped awkwardly up on to the plankwalk, he noticed for the first time that from the grimy windows and slatted doors of Ike Garvey's lamplit saloon there issued nothing but an eerie silence. That silence was explained when he pushed through those swing doors.

When they took him off his horse and carried him inside they had laid Marshal Lew Drummond on his sweat-stiffened horse blanket on the sawdust-covered dirt floor. He'd been

50

limp when his killers lashed him across his mount, stiff when he came off, so that cutting the rawhide bindings had not eased his position. He lay on his side, bent double at the waist, his arms stretched above his head like a man about to dive off a rock. His thinning hair was matted with blood. His stiff, encrusted shirt front was pocked with black holes.

A hatless Ed Thorpe, face streaked with dried blood, was leaning on the bar talking to big, burly Ike Garvey. The gambler who had raised the alarm was a little way away, leaning nonchalantly with his back to the bar, repeatedly riffling his deck of cards as he looked across at the table where the big bearded man, cheekbone gashed and swollen, was working his way with some distaste through a tall glass of Garvey's warm beer.

At McGill's approach, Thorpe swung around. At the same moment the swing doors slammed for a second time and Doc Lynch bustled in.

'Your signature on a paper's all that's needed, Doc,' Thorpe called bitterly and, as the sawbones grunted and knelt down alongside the dead lawman, the deputy turned to study McGill. 'What about your boy?'

'Come dawn tomorrow, Harper Wills'll take him up to boot-hill and bury him.'

'A kid,' Thorpe said, and his eyes were ugly. 'Tell me what the hell's goin' on, McGill, because it's got me baffled.'

'A warning,' McGill said, 'now this.' He walked to the bar, saw the pensive look in Thorpe's eyes and knew he was remembering their talk, the mention of three men forking mounts bearing the Spur brand, his scepticism. Well, now he'd seen for himself, tasted the violence, come close to death.

He collected the glass Garvey slid across the bar, tossed back the raw spirit, felt it hit like molten metal, its heat spread like a prairie fire. As he turned away with moist eyes, a horse snorted in the street, traces snapped and jingled, and he guessed Wills had arrived to collect the dead Spur rider. If he was Spur. And there was only one way of finding out.

'Two got away,' he said. 'You raisin' a posse?'

'It's customary,' Thorpe said.

'But?'

'Those two fellers went different ways. Maybe they came together outside town, maybe not. Even if they did, we can't be sure which way they headed.' He chewed his lip, cast a glance at the bearded man, said, 'I never did believe in chasin' rainbows, not when there's a quicker way.'

'So forget them. Ride with me to Spur.'

'Maybe. But not yet.'

He gestured to Ike Garvey, waited for him to fill two jolt glasses, then left the bar with them and slid into a chair across the table from the big man. As he pushed one glass across the table, Doc Lynch finished his business, snapped shut his leather case and walked out. Almost at once, two men came in, picked up the dead marshal and awkwardly carried him outside. Feet scraped on timber. Leather springs creaked. A man spoke softly. A wagon rolled.

'That could've been me comin' in belly down, takin' my last ride in Harper Wills' hearse,' Thorpe said, 'if Lew hadn't insisted huntin' down them horse-thieves was his job.'

'Life's full of ifs and maybes,' the big man acknowledged. He raised the glass to Thorpe, and both men drank.

'Gord Brady,' said the big man.

'Ed Thorpe. And I owe you some thanks.'

Brady grinned. 'After the way those two bested me?'

'Maybe I should throw your words back at you: most onlookers would say you did what you could, in the circumstances.'

'Most. But not you, and with good reason. Hell, I had first shot, and missed. That was inexcusable.'

'Or deliberate.'

The big man's blue eyes were amused. He'd discarded the mackinaw, and beneath the sleeves of his cotton shirt his upper arms bulged. 'That's the lawman talkin'. It's takin' you a while, but you're gettin' around to something,' he said.

McGill saw Thorpe purse his lips, hesitate. He picked up his fresh drink, left the bar, slid into the remaining chair. Thorpe glanced at him, put down the empty jolt glass, moodily twisted it between finger and thumb.

Without looking up, he said, 'This is Ewan McGill. Until today he ran a small spread on Cottonwood Creek. A couple of hours ago he came to me with a story, told me of threats, how his house had been burned to the ground, his wife gone missing. I regret that I only half listened. Now his boy's dead, two of the men in the mire up to their hocks are on the loose.'

He paused, looked up, waited, and when no comment was forthcoming said, 'Mister, you stepped into a fight when there was no need, and for that I've already thanked you. But, sore head or not, I couldn't help hearin' you call that lean feller by name. As to what conclusions I've reached, well, maybe your knowin' that feller's name puts a different light on your actions. You took my pistol, which seemed a clever stunt but put me out of the game. Then, when the time came for gunplay, you used that pistol but all you managed was to drill a fancy pattern of holes in Ike Garvey's wall.'

For a few moments Gord Brady was silent; not, so far as McGill could tell, deliberately holding back, but simply mulling over in his mind what had been said, maybe deciding whether the explosive events of the past hour gave Thorpe the right to ask questions not normally put to strangers.

The two men who had been divested of their weapons by the Spur riders had left hurriedly when the gunsmoke cleared. The gambler had moved away from the bar when a florid, cigar-smoking cattleman walked in and, after a brief conversation, he and the newcomer had moved to a corner table and were playing two-handed euchre. Ike Garvey was now up on a creaking stool probing the fresh bullet holes in the gilt-framed oil painting behind the bar and probably, McGill thought, bemoaning the fact that the recent gunplay had scared away the sparse Monday evening drinkers.

'Yeah, I knew them, after a fashion,' Brady said. 'Ran across 'em in Las Cruces, sat in on a game of fivecard draw, deuces wild — and at that time they was a foursome, Blade and Clete Skinner edgy and with one eye on their back-trail, Jeffers a hanger-on, all three of 'em leery of the hawkish character with the eyes of a killer. He'd rode in after me, said he'd come down through the Jornada Del Muerto. I'd been scrapin' a livin' in the Mogollons, got plumb wore out, crossed the Gila and was heading east with a small poke they did their damnedest to get their dirty paws on.'

He dug out the makings, rolled a cigarette, pinched the ends, scraped a match and lit up.

Through the haze of fresh smoke, Thorpe watched him toss the Bull Durham sack on the table, said carefully, 'Blade, Clete Skinner, Jeffers. That gives us three names . . .'

Ignoring the unspoken question, the big man said, 'After them mountains, I had a vague notion to cut across the plains and try San Antone. Still have, for that matter. And I wasn't averse to company. They mentioned they were makin' for Texas, so we rode down the Bravo as far as El Paso then on down to Fort Hancock before swinging east.'

'They say they were heading for Coyote Gulch?'

'Said nothing, but not too long after we left Hancock they showed a keen interest in a ranch set in a hollow high in the Sierra Blanca foothills. Diamond

K was the brand. Cattle every damn where.'

'Yeah, I've heard of the spread. So maybe that's what they were lookin for. They'd reached Texas, and it's the season when most ranchers are looking for top hands.'

'Seemed to me like their interest went beyond lookin' for work. Besides, we rode on. Took us a while to cross that range and ride out through the pass, mostly in what I'd define as a ruminative kind of silence. That night, around the fire, they shut me out, talked amongst themselves. The fourth feller — '

'The man with no name,' said Thorpe, wooden faced.

'Yeah, him, well, he was . . . ' — Brady squinted in thought — 'somewhat awestruck. Like a man seen that there Holy Grail, or its equivalent.'

'If he had,' Ewan McGill said, 'why would all four of them leave it behind and ride more than a hundred miles, cross the Apache Mountains and down to the Pecos then sign on to ride herd for Blake Seeger?

'Good question,' said Brady. 'But who's sayin' they did?'

'Sign on with Seeger?' McGill met the challenge in the intelligent blue eyes. 'I've crossed Skinner, Blade and Jeffers twice in three weeks. Both times all three men were riding Spur horses. Hell, you saw them.'

'Yeah,' Brady said, 'and your town marshal just got hisself killed huntin' down horse-thieves.'

'Them?' McGill said, unable to hide his disbelief. 'All three were right here in town.'

Ed Thorpe shook his head. 'You know they rode in at dusk, on your tail. There ain't no disputin' there's horse-thieves in the locality, and when Lew came in he'd been a long time dead.'

'All right,' McGill said. He glared at Thorpe and the big man, felt the hot anger stirring, his heart thumping. 'All right, let's look at that. They're horse-thieves. They ride all this way from New Mexico just so they can steal a few horses from Blake Seeger, from Darcy Griffin. Then, instead of movin' on, they order me off my spread and hang around Cottonwood Creek for three whole damn weeks.'

'And when he stays put,' Thorpe said softly, his eyes on Brady, 'they come back, burn down his house, grab a-hold of his wife and take her Christ knows where, gun down his kid.'

'Put like that,' Brady said, 'it don't make any kind of sense.'

'So what we do,' Thorpe said, 'is cut out the guesswork and look at the facts.'

McGill looked at Brady, then Thorpe, and shook his head helplessly. 'Three men ride down from New Mexico, pick on a man they've never set eyes on, drive him off a spread owned mostly by the Coyote Gulch bank.'

Thorpe grinned ironically at him. 'Yeah,' he said, 'that sounds much better.'

'Not three men,' Ike Garvey reminded

61

them. 'Four — or maybe five.'

He'd come around from behind the bar, for a while idly watched the euchre players, then dropped into a chair at a nearby table and fired up the stub of a cigar. His apron bulged over his belly; his moustaches fluttered under his bulbous nose as he puffed at the stogie, but his black, button eyes were bright and, from his long evenings around the poker table, McGill knew Ike Garvey for a man who said little but missed nothing.

'Those fellers rode through more than a month ago. Lookin' for work, they said, and them brands suggest they signed on at Spur. But this feller's right, there was four rode through,' Garvey went on, 'and if there ain't no sense in what them three fellers done, then maybe the fourth can give you some answers — if you can catch ahold of him.' He studied the end of his stogie, then flashed a shrewd glance at Thorpe. 'And while you're at it,' he said, 'consider this: you're listenin' to a fifth stranger's story, and swallowin' it like it was gospel.'

'Where I come from,' Brady said, 'that's known as blackening a man's character — '

'Or cuttin' through the bullshit,' Thorpe cut in. 'Which is what I'd like you to do.' He glared at Brady, reached for the big man's tobacco sack and fashioned a cigarette with strong, impatient fingers that threatened to tear the paper to shreds.

'All right,' Brady said. 'Five of us rode in, but I was always an outsider so when four went on to the Pecos I stayed in town. In that time, I've been making enquiries.'

'And?'

'A wire from the land office at Fort Hancock informs me that the owner of the big spread we rode through — the Diamond K — recently pegged out.'

'Go on.' Thorpe trickled smoke, slid the Bull Durham across to the bearded man.

'His name was Earl J. Ketchum. The family had split up, his wife left him and moved to California where she died. Accordin' to a lawyer the land office put me on to, Ketchum neglected to leave a will.'

McGill felt his breath catch, turned the faint sound into a deliberate clearing of the throat. He saw Thorpe sense something, glance quickly at him, then back at Brady. The bearded man had also caught the sudden tension.

'That middle initial interests me, because I don't believe in coincidence,' he said. 'Up in Las Cruces, when I was sittin' across the poker table from the feller with killer's eyes, they mostly addressed him as Stretch, once or twice changed that to Jack.' He paused, pocketed his tobacco sack. 'That made his initial J. And I already had his second name.'

'Which, even though you ain't so far told us,' Ed Thorpe said, 'don't leave any need to make wild guesses. Over the years, Jack 'Stretch' Ketchum's name's cropped up in connection with crimes as far apart as Arizona and Montana. Right now, there's a price on his head across the border in Mexico. And if Earl J. Ketchum *was* his father, then his interest in the Diamond K ain't no surprise. With his pa dead, he's a rich man.'

'Maybe,' McGill said hoarsely.

'Ain't no maybe about it,' Brady said. 'Another question I asked was if Earl J. had more than one son.' He shook his head. 'He didn't.'

McGill took a deep breath. 'You asked the wrong question: what you should have asked was did he have more than one child. I think he did.'

'What makes you say that?' Ed Thorpe said. 'Which is probably a stupid question because the logical answer seems to be screamin' at me.'

'My wife's past life has been a closed book. She'd never tell me why, but that's the way she's always wanted it, and I've honoured her wishes,' McGill said. 'About the only thing I do know is her maiden name — and, yeah, that was Ketchum. Knowing that, everything that's been going on hereabouts falls into place. If she's Earl J.'s oldest child and there's no will, with her mother dead the Diamond K will go to her, and this feller Stretch won't get a bean.' He smiled, but it was a twisted smile in which there was no pleasure. 'Stretch Ketchum's intention must be to get rid of Verity and her entire family, wiping out the line of inheritance — and it looks like he's two thirds of the way there.'

5

They had to start someplace, Ed Thorpe said, so why not ride out to Spur, talk with Blake Seeger? Although it had been his suggestion at the start, this acceptance of the notion at first surprised McGill, who had Thorpe down as a man with sceptic for a middle name squeezed in between hefty measures of common sense and caution.

Common sense made it obvious, after what they had learned or surmised, that Blake Seeger had no hand in the threats, the torching of McGill's house or the killing of his son but, after some consideration, McGill could understand the way Thorpe's mind was working.

The killers were riding Spur mounts. They'd been around Coyote Gulch for more than a month. Maybe they did sign on with Spur. The bunkhouse would be a handy place to untie their bedrolls; with the spring roundups not yet started they'd have some free time, and as Spur hands they were no longer drifters and would have a pat answer if questions were asked.

If, on the other hand, they'd raided Seeger's remuda, then he'd be keen to know of developments, and might have useful information to contribute.

Brady declined Thorpe's invitation to ride along with them, and clumped upstairs to his room above Garvey's saloon with a whiskey bottle dangling from his big fist and the lawman's openly suspicious stare boring into his broad back. But Jake Harding heard the goings on, came running across from his store to listen more closely, and five minutes after the meeting broke up he was back astride his rangy sorrel with his hat tugged down and a replacement shotgun tucked into the saddle boot.

McGill's only lingering concern was for his son. Harding put his mind at a kind of uneasy rest by telling him that his wife, Min, would willingly make arrangements for the funeral and ensure that it took place the next morning. Not ideal, for McGill knew that if they learned anything or nothing at Spur, he would press on and pursue the killers, if need be to the ends of the earth. Missing his boy's funeral was a small price to pay if his death could be avenged — and there was also the small matter of Verity, out there, somewhere, in the hands of Jack 'Stretch' Ketchum.

There was grim determination in his whole demeanour as he, Jake Harding and Ed Thorpe rode up main street and in a short while left the lights of Coyote Gulch twinkling hazily through the dust of their passing.

★　★　★

Seeger's Double Spur ranch was a sprawling building flanked by barns and outbuildings set in a hollow fringed by aspens a mile or so from the Pecos river. Moonlight glinted on the distant water. Cottonwood trees were indistinct grey shapes, ghostly in the pale light.

It was gone two in the morning when McGill, Thorpe and Harding rode down from the higher ground and across the short grass and under the heavy cross beam burned with the Spur brand, but lights still gleamed in the windows of the house and, in the long, low bunkhouse, a man was singing softly to a tinkling guitar.

A cigarette glowed in the shadows alongside the lamplit windows as they skirted the corral and clattered across the hard-packed yard. When they drew near to the house, swung down and hitched their horses, Blake Seeger had moved across the wide gallery and was at the top of the steps.

'Jake, Ed?' he said quietly, and under a shock of white hair a slight frown creased his unlined brow.

'Looks bad, us comin' at this hour, but there's no trouble,' Thorpe said. 'Leastwise, nothing for you to fret over.'

'Thought maybe you'd caught those rascals, brought back my horses.'

'Ah,' Thorpe said. 'That answers one question without the bother of askin'.'

And now McGill felt the power of the rawboned rancher's gaze. He nodded, saw the shadow of a smile flit across a countenance that was all planes and angles, then Seeger turned away.

'Come on into the house, all of you.'

They followed him through the wide doorway into a living room darkly furnished and elegantly draped with buffalo rugs and bright Indian blankets. Lamplight pooled on glossy tables, spilled over on to a scrubbed board floor. Rifles gleamed in racks. Oil paintings were sombre on peeled log walls.

'My wife's asleep upstairs, I'm still up and about only because a birthday shindig over at the bunkhouse kept me awake.' Seeger turned to face them, gestured to seats, took a decanter from a cabinet and tilted it high for the liquor to catch the light. 'The young

71

feller with the guitar has had too much of some strong hooch vaguely resembling this. He'll fall sleep, or die. I can offer you a little, but of better quality.'

The drinks poured into crystal glasses and passed around, he settled into a leather swivel chair turned away from a heavy desk, sipped the fine whiskey and looked at Thorpe.

'One question suggests more to come, Ed. The gash on your head tells me they're likely to be of some importance. Jake's being here is no surprise, he's got his nose into most things' — this with a grin at the storekeeper — 'but Ewan McGill wouldn't be with you unless my answers are likely to concern him in some way.'

'The horses stolen from you gave me some wrong ideas,' McGill said, and he caught himself wondering how he could possibly have believed that this polite, amusing man was the cause of his troubles. 'If you got wind of them, I apologize now — but I need to know more about those thieves.'

'For reasons that get kinda complicated, they threatened him some three weeks ago. Yesterday they burned down his house, murdered his boy,' Thorpe said, and McGill saw genuine shock in the lean rancher's eyes, the bony hand tighten on the glass. 'Verity McGill's gone missing, and them reasons I mentioned make it clear she's in mortal danger.' Thorpe paused, thought for a moment, then said, 'The horses they rode pointed suspicion in this direction, so I'd be interested to hear when they was taken.'

Seeger sighed. 'Yesterday,' he said, then glanced across the room at a long-case clock and said, 'No, it's past midnight so make that the day before. All four of them rode — '

'Four?'

'Mmm. I signed three on together, the fourth feller rode in some time after, maybe a day or so before they all turned horse-thief.' He glanced at McGill. 'And if you were threatened three weeks ago, then your suspicions were justified. At that time, three of them were Spur riders.'

'Moot point,' Jake Harding growled. 'They never had no intention of doin' any damn range work.'

'But what they did intend is complicated?'

McGill shook his head. 'Not any more. The figurin' took some time, but what it boils down to is a rich feller called Earl J. Ketchum dyin' and his ranch goin' to his next of kin. Verity's maiden name was Ketchum — '

'The fourth man went by that name,' Seeger cut in, and Thorpe nodded.

'Right. Jack Ketchum.'

'The others were Blade Devlin, Clete Skinner, Luke Jeffers,' Seeger said, and waited expectantly.

'Jeffers is dead. Devlin and Skinner made it out of town.'

'I know Verity,' Seeger said. 'I'd guess she's a mite older than the man Ketchum — her brother? — so she should inherit. But what now?'

'Anything you can give us,' Thorpe said. 'Three weeks on your spread. They must've said something to somebody.'

'Not so.' Seeger shook his head. 'You ever hear a chuckline rider shoot his mouth off? And from what you've said these fellers had something to hide.'

'And the day before yesterday,' McGill said, 'they lit out?'

'Well before dawn.'

'All four?'

'Sure.' Seeger cocked an eyebrow.

Thorpe shrugged. 'If that's so, they split up. Ketchum wasn't with them in town.'

Seeger nodded slowly. 'Then he's got McGill's wife.'

'Yeah,' Jake Harding said. 'But where?'

'And why?' said McGill.

In the silence, the long-case clock ticked the seconds away, its beat a soothing counterpoint to the faint tinkle of the guitar. McGill had asked the question, but in his heart he knew the answer. Jack Ketchum had not balked at getting rid of McGill and his boy, but how could he murder his own sister? In cold blood? Clearly, because Verity had wiped her past life off the slate, there had been a family bust up. It seemed to McGill that what Ketchum had done was take her somewhere so they could talk, leaving the killing to Devlin, Jeffers and Skinner. That left him in the clear, innocent of any crime; their word against his. If he could talk Verity round from the smouldering, deep-rooted anger over whatever dispute had split the family, then with her husband and son dead it would be reasonable for her to return with him to the Diamond K. They were sister and brother. It was in a woman's nature to care for her menfolk.

'The way I see it,' Jake Harding said, watching him closely, 'the whys can be pondered over when the time's right — and that ain't now.'

'And if they kept their lips buttoned the whole time they were at Spur,'

Thorpe said, 'then this is the wrong place to go diggin' for answers.'

'I wish I could be of more help,' Seeger said, and frowned. 'Maybe there was talk that never reached my ears. One man who might know is my foreman, Eddie Marr.'

'He around?'

'He rode out with the wrangler a couple of days ago, gathering loose broncs, checking line cabins.' He smiled wryly at the deputy. 'He comes across those ruffians they'll have some story ready, and no reason for him to disbelieve. But if Verity McGill's with them . . .'

McGill made a hard, impatient sound at the back of his throat. 'Like Ed says, we're doin' our diggin' in the wrong place, and Christ knows we've got precious little time.' He stood up, moved restlessly to the big window, swung around. 'Ed, you say Jack Ketchum's been ridin' the wrong side of the law for some years. Accordin' to Gord Brady, he came down out of central New Mexico, and on the way here all four of them rode straight by the Diamond K.'

'Suggests he was hell bent on gettin' you and your family out of the way,' Harding said, 'before ridin' back like the prodigal son to claim his inheritance.'

'If he was in such a damned hurry,' Ed Thorpe said, 'why wait three weeks?'

'Maybe that wasn't the plan,' McGill said. 'Ketchum knew he couldn't show his face or Verity would have recognized him. I'm also pretty sure he can't bring himself to kill her. Seems to me Jeffers, Devlin and Skinner had orders to scare us off, but when time dragged on and I was refusin' to back down, Ketchum was forced to step in. Quickest way to make us move was to burn us out.'

'He let them three do the dirty work,' Harding said, 'and when they rode away from the blaze with Verity in the buckboard, Jack Ketchum appeared from out of nowhere so she knew her fine upstanding brother had rescued her from black-hearted owlhoots.'

Thorpe nodded. 'Only trouble was, they chose a day when McGill and his boy were in the hills.'

'And that left work to be finished in town,' Harding said.

'Half finished,' McGill said and, as he moved to the cabinet with his empty glass, he felt the muscles bunch in his jaw.

'If Ketchum rode in nigh on three weeks after his cronies,' Seeger said thoughtfully, 'he must have camped somewhere.'

'Or holed up,' Ewan McGill said. 'In a line cabin.'

Seeger shot him a look. 'Possible. They've been empty all winter. If he did, that's where he'll take your wife.'

Thorpe sighed, shook his head. 'Next step is we ride out, see if surmisin' turns out to be fact. Problem is, I've got business in town. With Lew Drummond dead, the town council'll be lookin' for a new marshal. Likely to be me, so I'll need to see Mayor John

Moore and sort that out, get a deputy sworn in . . . '

'Two of us can handle it,' Jake Harding said, and winked at McGill.

'Add a Spur rider or two and the odds'd be more favourable,' said Thorpe, not hiding his misgivings. He threw a questioning look at Seeger.

'Wish I could,' said the rancher, 'but — '

'No,' Ewan McGill said. 'You've already got two men out there could run into trouble. That's enough.'

'And enough talk,' Jake Harding said. He was out of his seat, a man built like a gnarled tree, his eyes like cold steel.

As they walked out ahead of Blake Seeger, paused in the cool of the covered gallery to look out at the hazy orb of the waning moon, Ed Thorpe turned his gaze to the north-west and said, 'Devlin and Skinner are out there somewhere. They'll want to finish the job. But it's not them bothers me.'

'Who, then?' McGill said. 'Gord Brady?'

'I'll look in Garvey's saloon when I get back,' Ed Thorpe said. 'If that big man's still upstairs, it'll be my surprise for the day.'

'He told a good story. Why should he lie?'

'I told him I knew of the Diamond K. What I'd heard is, Earl J. Ketchum got to be big by treading on toes. A lot of the men he hired were more familiar with six-guns than ropes. Now, what if Gord Brady was one of those men? What if Brady went lookin' for Stretch Ketchum, told him the old man had pegged out and the ranch could be his, offered his help — at a price?'

'Then Ike Garvey was right,' Harding said. 'They're all in it together.'

'And if I'm right,' Ed Thorpe said, 'and he ain't in his room when I get back, then the man who could be the wild card in as loco a deck as I've come across is runnin' loose and as dangerous as a rogue longhorn.'

6

'You're not making sense,' Verity McGill said.

'You think about it,' said Jack Ketchum. 'Your home's gone, burned to the ground. Pa's dead. Diamond K's there, biggest spread west of the Pecos, settin' waitin' for the two of us — '

'For me. Ma died years ago. If Pa's dead, Diamond K's mine.'

'But you need a man to run it, I'm your brother — '

'You damn fool, I've got a husband, a child.'

'Maybe.'

The sudden silence in the cabin was electric. A frisson of shock rippled through Verity, and she felt the hairs lift on her neck, the blood drain from her face.

'What . . . what the hell do you mean?'

They had argued back and forth all morning. Jack Ketchum was sitting on a wooden chair by the table, his back to the small window lit by the blazing light of the midday sun. His long legs were stretched out, heels resting on the box of logs alongside the cold iron stove. There was a look of cynical amusement on his lean face, but the eyes that were still the part of him most familiar to her, were devoid of emotion, and Verity knew they would stay that way; knew that whatever answer he gave would be calculated, and only lightly sprinkled with truth.

Then the thin smile was wiped out, to be replaced by a look of concern.

'I snatched you from those owlhoots, Verity, saved your life and you know it.'

'Yes, but what were you doing there?'

'You know damn well what. I heard Pa died, so I came lookin' for the sister I haven't seen for ten, twelve years —'

'And cared nothing for, even then.

83

Never played where I played, never went with me to secret places like kids do.'

'I was keen to get out in the world.'

'And you did. But the scent of money brought you back and I suppose I'm lucky you found me when you did. Or was it luck? Maybe you're in cahoots — '

'Hell, now who's not makin' sense? I don't know who they are or why they burned your spread.'

'We were warned off. By men riding Spur horses.'

'Big local ranch?'

'A powerful, decent man who has never leaned on us. So those warnings, too, make no sense.' And she challenged him with her eyes, standing in the centre of the tiny line cabin with her arms folded and her legs braced and a heart fluttering like that of a frightened jack-rabbit.

'Range barons get a sudden itch to expand.' He shrugged. 'All the more reason you should move away, take over

84

a spread that don't get stepped on by — '

'And what about Ewan? What about my boy, Johnny?'

'Putting your house to the torch,' he said, pinning her with his cold eyes, 'was just the start.'

'Oh, God!'

She turned away, biting her lip, stared blankly at the raw log walls, the tilting shelves with their rusting tins, the bunk with its bare cornhusk mattress, the coiled lass-ropes, the saddles and mildewed bridles . . . the thick dust . . . and she thought about her bright, tidy home and knew her heart would break if anything happened to . . .

'You're wrong,' she said huskily. 'Ewan's too strong for them.'

'A strong man can't fight a lead slug, fired from a Spencer he don't even see.'

'You know that's how it'll be?' She swung on him, her eyes blazing. 'You know — or you're guessing? Which is it, Jack?'

'Hell, it's just I've seen it happen

when men get range hungry. A couple of warnings, they ain't heeded, then one day the squatter's found with a bullet in his back and — '

'I've heard enough, I'm leaving.'

'Goin' where?'

'Coyote Gulch. I've got friends who'll know what to do. They'll help me.'

'But I need your help.'

Her laugh was brittle. 'The Diamond K is yours. I give it to you, with my blessing.'

'Maybe it ain't that easy.'

'Why not?'

Again he shrugged. 'There's lawyers involved.'

'So?'

And now the cold eyes were hooded, the phoney look of concern that had failed to sway her subtly transformed so that the cadaverous face became a pale, glistening mask of menace, the white teeth wolf-like as the thin lips parted.

'I guess news of my . . . exploits . . . ain't reached your tender ears, little sister.'

'Ah.' She nodded sudden understanding. 'You're wrong; I have heard,
and seen the Wanted dodgers. You can't
walk into a lawyer's office, can you,
maybe not even ride into Fort Hancock? You'd be arrested. So it's not as a
partner you want me; without me there
to handle the paperwork, you can't
possibly take over the Diamond K.'

He grinned. 'That about sums it up.'

'Well that's tough, Jack, because I
told you, I'm leaving.'

'No.'

Face set, eyes narrowed, she suddenly
darted towards the door and his boots
slammed on the dirt floor as he
uncoiled from the chair with the speed
of a striking rattler. As one long stride
took him across the slanting sunlight
and into her path and she slammed into
his hard chest and felt fingers like iron
bear traps clamp painfully on the
muscles of her upper arms, there came
the sudden rattle of hooves, the
murmur of voices, the wet sound of
tired horses blowing.

'Ewan,' she said, her eyes on his, feeling his sour breath warm and moist on her face. 'I told you he was too strong.' And with a swift jerk she tore herself free, stepped back, and looked expectantly towards the door.

Part Two

DRY-GULCHED

7

McGill and Harding rode west with Ed Thorpe for five miles then left him and cut north across the scrub until the harsh smell of burning timber was in their nostrils and they circled the cold black embers of the house, eerily phosphorescent in the darkness, and rode in silence down the trail until they reached the abandoned buckboard.

By that time, the moon was little more than a disc of the palest gossamer floating above a purple smudge of hills in skies that bore the promise of the approaching dawn. It was in that half light that Jake Harding swung down, hitched his mount to the wagon and began quartering the ground.

They had learned from Blake Seeger as they mounted up in his yard that Spur used two line cabins, one fifteen miles to the north, another about the same distance to the south. Both cabins lay on a line roughly ten miles to the east of Spur. They were gambling everything on Verity being held in one of them.

But which one?

While Harding studied the tracks left by Devlin, Jeffers and Skinner — and, if they had things figured right, by Jack Ketchum — McGill tied his horse then leaned awkwardly against the wagon with a cigarette glowing in his cupped hand. In the pre-dawn hours the air was chill. His coat was on, the collar tugged up around his ears. He was tilted a little to one side: his thigh had begun to ache, the puffed, lacerated flesh irritated and restricted by the rough cloth of his pants. But the ache in his mind was a thousand times worse, for he knew that finding Verity was the easy part of that night's work, telling her of her loss something he could hardly bear to contemplate.

Harding returned to the wagon, his eyes glinting with triumph.

'They headed north,' he said, and McGill nodded.

'Yeah, that's the way it looked to me when I rode by at sunset, but I had Johnny with me so . . . ' He flicked the cigarette away angrily.

'You ain't asked me the whole story.'

'From lookin' at a patch of dirt? Hell, I had you down as a storekeeper, not an Injun.'

'Must be a bit of both in there,' Harding said. 'From them tracks I can make out clear enough three came here with the buckboard. Another rider came fast out of the scrub. Three riders scattered, then the lone rider turned round and rode north. But he had another rider with him, and that horse was the one that was pullin' the buckboard.'

'Verity,' McGill said. 'He made her ride bareback. Sounds like a mighty considerate brother.'

'Maybe he gave her his horse,' Harding said, and laughed. 'Anyhow, there was a lot goin' on but you know what happened to those riders that scattered: you came through with Johnny, and they regrouped and hung on your tail. Then, clearest of all, overlayin' those tracks, we've got two riders coming fast from the direction of town. They hung around for a while, then rode off in the same direction: north.'

'Devlin and Skinner?'

'Who else? And what does it tell us? Maybe Ketchum rode a-ways north but holed up with Verity in these woods until they got back from town. Maybe they ain't never used no cabin, and right now they're halfway to Diamond K. Or maybe Ketchum pulled a fast one, lit out with your wife.' His grin was bleak. 'Maybe a whole lot of things that don't do us any damn good . . . ' His voice trailed away, and with a grunt of disgust he fumbled his corncob out of a pocket and began packing it with tobacco.

'But the only maybe we've got to hang on to,' McGill said, 'is maybe

Ketchum did use that cabin — and that's where we're goin'.'

A match flared, Harding puffed at his pipe then went to the horses with smoke streaming over his shoulder. There was the smooth sound of metal on oiled leather. When he turned around, McGill saw he was holding a Spencer rifle.

'Picked it up in the street, damn thing near broke my wrist so I figured I'd paid that black-eyed sonofabitch for it.' He held it out. 'If we do come across Skinner, you might get some pleasure out of payin' him in kind.'

The sour taste of bile was in McGill's throat as he took hold of the long rifle that had killed his son.

'He fired more than once,' he said. 'Maybe it's out of shells.'

'You're forgettin' I run a store,' Harding said. 'I reloaded, but if you need more there's a box in my saddle-bag.' He grinned. 'I also brung a second Spencer so we're usin' the same shells.'

'Goddamn!' McGill said softly. 'Here's me still totin' your pistol — can't even recall where I mislaid mine — and you're doin' all my thinking, all the work. You reckon I'm safe to be with, out there in the woods?'

Harding chuckled, clapped him on the shoulder. 'Between us, feller, we'll scrape through.'

'I hope you're right — but there's one other 'maybe' you never mentioned.'

'That being?'

'Skinner and Devlin murdered my boy, but that was only half of it. Maybe they're out there now, hunkered on the high ground somewhere along that fifteen mile of open country between here and the cabin, waitin' for me to go after them so's they can finish the job.'

Harding tapped his pipe against his boot, ground the glowing tobacco into the hard earth with his heel. Then he straightened, and spat.

'They're doin' that, by now they'll be gettin' cold and impatient.' His level gaze measured McGill, and he said softly, 'You wouldn't want to disappoint them, would you?'

'Skinner shot down my boy. If I'm right, the two of them are standing between me and Verity,' McGill said, and swung decisively towards his horse. 'Let's ride, Jake.'

★ ★ ★

The sun's dazzling orb had floated high above the eastern horizon and was burning fiercely on the land, as Clete Skinner and Blade Devlin rode into the shallow arroyo and followed its snaking course until the dry wash widened into a broad hollow, where huge, fallen boulders lay against rocky sides, and gnarled cottonwoods and deadwood were as grey as the arid dust at its centre.

The clatter of hooves changed to a muted thudding as they emerged from the rocky confines on to the hard earth and parched grass of that open space, and the black-garbed killer on the horse stolen from Blake Seeger's Double Spur twisted his head around to grin at Blade Devlin.

'We won't find a better place.'

Devlin lifted the reins, slowed, let his horse wheel and back under the bridle then leaned forward to touch its neck as it tossed its head and the bit clinked.

'We could wait all day, and McGill never show. I thought the idea was to put distance between us while he wastes time at Spur.'

'Happens we've got time to kill,' Skinner said, and grinned at the double meaning in his words as he slipped out of the saddle. 'And Stretch wants that time at the cabin to tell a story, try to talk that gal around. We ride in too soon, he'll blow his top.'

'I'm shakin' in my boots,' Devlin said, and Skinner laughed.

'Tell me again,' Devlin said. 'What happens if she spits in his eye?'

'The way Stretch tells it, she rides to

Fort Hancock anyway, only the pretence is done with.' He shrugged. 'Myself, I never could see that happenin'.'

Devlin stepped down, stretched, eased his shoulders.

'Goddamn pretence!' He gathered the reins, held them in gloved hands, scowled at Clete Skinner. 'There's a lawyer over at Hancock growin' whiskers while he sets there holdin' a pen and a piece of paper worth a fortune.'

'He'll get a signature,' Skinner said, 'one way or another.'

'And then?'

'Like I said, we'll do what it takes.'

Devlin frowned. 'If Diamond K's goin' to us in the end, and the girl's the only one can sign, who needs Stretch?'

Skinner leaned his elbows on the saddle, tipped back his black Stetson, scratched his greasy hair and looked across his horse at Devlin.

'That's an easy one: when you get right down to it, nobody needs him. But right now he's callin' the shots, so there's tougher questions need answerin'. Like, given the chance, will Stretch talk her round, get his hands on that spread nice an' easy like he wants to? And if she does spit in his eye, how's he gonna make her walk into that office and sign? With a price on his head, there's no way he can take her in with a gun at her back. If he did try it that way, the lawyer would take one look and put the goddamn paper back in his safe. So if that wouldn't work, what hold's he got on her to make her do it on her own?' He shook his head. 'He ain't thinkin' straight. He's set on wipin' out her family, when he could've used them to twist her arm.'

'Maybe,' Devlin said, 'we should do it for him? Grab ourselves a hole card, make that little gal dance to our tune?'

Skinner's grin was wicked. He looked up at the skies, then jerked a thumb and both men led their horses across the grass to the tumbled boulders up against the east wall of the arroyo. Shadows there were deep, even with the sun at its highest. And the outlook down the arroyo was like looking across a wide meadow into a narrow funnel out of which a rider would emerge totally exposed.

A jagged outcrop provided a high wall behind which their horses would be hidden. Skinner led his in, ground hitched it and quickly fixed a hobble. When he straightened, Blade Devlin had slipped his Winchester out of its boot and was squinting at him, a question in his narrowed eyes.

'What I say make sense? Or not?'

Skinner's black eyes were amused. 'Yeah, only now it's you ain't thinkin' straight. We plug McGill, he's out of the way permanent, can't never walk in and stake his claim to that ranch. So why risk grabbin' ourselves a live hole card?'

Devlin grinned, noisily worked the lever on the Winchester, said happily, 'Keep talkin', pard, I can see where this is leadin'.'

'Yeah, think about it. McGill's dead, but when we walk into that cabin, there's only you and me know that. Just like there's only you and me know Luke Jeffers never made it out of Coyote Gulch. So we take Stretch to one side, tell him Luke's holdin' Ewan McGill.'

'And when Verity McGill hears what's goin' on, she knows if she don't ride into Hancock and sign them papers,' Devlin said, 'she'll never see her husband alive.'

'Right. So now we draw straws. My Spencer's lyin' in the dust back in Coyote Gulch. That Winchester's gonna provide us with a nice, safe way of sendin' that gal to Hancock. But only one of us can pull the trigger.'

Five minutes later, they had left their hobbled horses grazing on the short grass behind the outcrop and settled down under cover of the boulders. The Winchester was propped against a rock alongside Clete Skinner. Blade Devlin was working on his six-gun, checking the loads and the action but knowing well that the back-up it provided would not be needed. Skinner would take

McGill with a single shot. If he had other men with him, they would die.

Skinner drank from his water bottle, corked it, tossed it to Devlin.

'Killin' McGill will give us a lever to use on his wife,' he said, 'but somewhere out there there's a wild card that don't make me too happy.'

'Gord Brady?'

'Yeah.' Skinner picked up the rifle, slammed it to his shoulder, took a practice sighting across the arroyo. 'I never did trust that man. But maybe he'll be ridin' alongside McGill,' he said, and then, squinting, still drawing a bead on the opening to the narrow passage through the arroyo, he hooked his finger around the trigger and said softly and with deadly menace, 'Pow! Pow!'

8

An hour after partaking of a late breakfast, John Moore, mayor and leader of Coyote Gulch's town council, swore in Ed Thorpe as the new town marshal and strode purposefully with him across the street to the saloon to drag a grumbling Ike Garvey out of bed at what, for him, was an early hour.

In the dim, cool interior, the two officials ceremoniously knocked back a shot glass of Ike Garvey's special reserve Kentucky whiskey that was brought reluctantly from under the timber bar, that drink being, in part, a celebration of Thorpe's elevated staus, and most definitely a remembrance of the departed Lew Drummond.

While Garvey, using his early awakening as a chance to get things done, called in the bleary-eyed swamper and the floor was swept and liberally covered with fresh sawdust, Moore raised the vexing question of a deputy.

'You always were the best man we could find for the job, Ed,' he said, 'and with you moved up a step it's going to be difficult to fill your shoes.'

Moore was short, fat, and immaculately dressed, and had a perpetually worried appearance that was a cover for his impressive intelligence and efficiency.

'Could do worse than old Mose,' Garvey said, wooden-faced, from behind the bar, jerking a thumb at the swamper who was bald, gap-toothed and not entirely in possession of all his faculties. The old man grinned wetly, and promptly tripped over a chair.

Hiding a grin, Ed Thorpe said, 'Deputy marshal ain't exactly the job folk fall over themselves to get. One minute you're catchin' stray dogs, the next you're dodgin' stray bullets — and the pay ain't exactly generous.'

'Best we can do,' Moore said, sticking out his chin, and Thorpe nodded, then turned his head as boots thumped overhead and Gord Brady appeared at the top of the stairs.

The big man came stomping down with a frown like thunder clouding the bearded face that bore the scars of his recent clash with Blade Devlin, crossed the floor to plant his tied bedroll on the bar and gesture to Ike Garvey.

'Bar's closed,' Garvey said, and turned his back to polish the big mirror with wide sweeps of a filthy rag.

Brady looked pointedly at the two empty glasses in front of Moore and Thorpe.

'Special occasion,' Moore said.

'I got me the marshal's badge,' Thorpe said, watching Brady, 'so if there's anything you want to add to your story — or maybe take back — I'm willing to listen.'

'Take back?'

'Wasn't most of what you told me a pack of lies?'

The big man pursed his lips. 'If I . . . bent the truth . . . it was in the reason for my actions. But I was in Las Cruces, met them four, rode down with them exactly like I said.'

'Why?'

'My brother lives and works in Fort Hancock. After a long spell away I moved close to home, spent twelve months as Diamond K ramrod, got thrown out when I mouthed off about Earl Ketchum's crooked ways stickin' in my craw.'

'No scrapin' a living in the Mogollons, no itch to try San Antone?'

The big man shrugged. 'It gave those fellers a good reason for me bein' up there in New Mexico. Not the real one — '

'That bein'?'

'Well, you already know the old man died. And word was, young Jack Ketchum was about to come in off the owlhoot and take over where his old man left off.'

John Moore was nodding slowly. 'I don't know what you told Ed, but from what you're saying now there can be only one logical reason why you'd ride with those men instead of just walking away from Diamond K.'

Brady nodded agreement. 'It was my intention — hell, it still is — to keep a close watch on Jack Ketchum. My instincts always were against him takin' over because, with her mother dead, Verity's the legal heir to the spread. But if Earl J.'s death brings brother and sister together, and they can sort out their differences and work side by side . . . '

Thorpe grunted. 'Ain't likely. Eyes of a killer, you said.'

'Yeah.' Brady frowned, remembering. 'I could be wrong, but if that's the way he turns out, then I'll make damn sure he don't get within a hundred miles of that ranch. Place is already run down. Cattle're running wild, every damn hand quit when the old man died. Ketchum'd let it stay like that.'

'Easiest way of keepin' him away,' Ike Garvey growled, a stogie fired up under his bushy moustache, 'would be to've plugged him stone daid soon's you set eyes on him.'

Brady shook his head. 'That'd be Earl Ketchum's way. And it would have made no difference.'

'It would have saved young Johnny McGill,' Ed Thorpe said.

Again, Brady shook his head. 'No.'

Moore said, 'No, it wouldn't. To save that boy you would have had to kill them all — isn't that right?'

'Yeah, I can see that,' Ed Thorpe said thoughtfully. 'Diamond K's high up in the Singin' Hills, close to the Mex border. For owlhoots, it'd be the next best thing to Hole in the Wall.'

Moore raised an eyebrow. 'Singing Hills?'

'Something about the winds up there. Injuns reckon when they blow from a certain direction, at a certain time . . . ' Thorpe shrugged.

In the sudden silence, Ike Garvey reached behind him, slammed a bottle on the bar and set four glasses tinkling alongside it. While Garvey poured, Ed

Thorpe began fashioning a cigarette. John Moore took his drink to a nearby table and sat down, Gord Brady joined him and dropped his bedroll at his feet.

'What I still don't understand, Brady,' Ed Thorpe said, 'is your interest in this.'

'I told you wires had been goin' back and to between me and a lawyer in Fort Hancock. That wasn't true, because there was no need: he's Verity Ketchum's uncle. Like me, he knows the Ketchums' story, knows about the big bust up that came about because Earl Ketchum's own family got sick of his crooked ways — and he knows Verity's the legal heir to Diamond K.'

'That explains this lawyer feller's interest,' Ed Thorpe said. 'I asked about yours.'

'His name's Mike Brady.'

Thorpe's eyes widened. '*He's* your brother?'

Brady nodded.

'So if Verity Ketchum — McGill — is his niece, she's also yours?'

'Right. Earl Ketchum is my brother-in-law.'

'I guess,' John Moore said quietly, 'we've just found ourselves that new deputy marshal.'

9

The first slug hummed like an angry hornet in the hot, still air, hit with a meaty thump to take McGill's horse from under him and, as the vicious crack reached his ears, sent him crashing with a jarring thud to the hard packed earth. The second bullet clipped Jake Harding's saddle-horn as he wrenched the reins over and set off at full gallop across the sun-drenched hollow and away from the curling wisp of gunsmoke that identified the bushwhacker's position.

McGill's horse kicked once, then its dying breath gusted and it lay still. High on the rimrock, a bird screeched angrily. Flies buzzed. Dislodged by the thunder of gunfire, a stone rattled its way down the rocky walls. Gritting his teeth, McGill rolled on to his belly and wriggled into the shadows. As he squinted into the sunlight, he saw a haze of dust drift across the wide hollow; heard again the crack of the rifle as the hidden gunman sent a shot winging after Jake Harding.

Too late, McGill thought with satisfaction. Jake had fooled them, and gone to ground.

'If there's an ambush,' McGill had warned his friend as they looked warily ahead to where sunlight blazed into the rocky opening, 'it'll come as we ride out into Jackson's Hole.'

'All right,' the Coyote Gulch store owner had said, 'seein' as there ain't no way round and you ain't goin' back, we'll come out of this arroyo like outlaw stallions out of a chute gate.'

And they'd done that, putting spurs to their mounts as the confining walls fell away and, in a sudden clatter of hoofs, had exploded out into the sunlight so fast the bushwhacker had been taken completely by surprise. That his first snap shot had taken McGill's horse was a tribute to the gunman's skill and marksmanship. But he had intended to kill a man, and he'd failed.

Now, McGill figured, all bets were off as Jake Harding took cover on the far side of the hollow and the bushwhackers — for, sure as hell there were two of them there, Skinner and Devlin — found themselves facing the shock of armed men in a position to pin them down with a deadly crossfire.

If, that was, McGill could get his hands on the big Spencer wedged under the dead weight of his horse. As its legs buckled, the big sorrel's momentum had carried it down the gentle incline. Far enough, McGill estimated, for him to offer a clear target to the bushwhacker if he went after that gun.

Risky. And this was for Verity. Gutsy as she was, if she was still alive she would by now be desperate, waiting for him, praying for him. So if he couldn't reach that rifle then, by God, he'd have to work his way close, get within range so he could use Jake's Colt.

Even as those thoughts ran through his mind, Harding's rifle cracked and sparks flew away to McGill's right as a slug spanged off a boulder and whined into the blue. A second shot followed the first and, as the hidden rifle opened up in reply and shots were exchanged across the hollow, McGill scrambled to his feet and made it to the dead sorrel in a crouching run. The Spencer's stock was poking out from under the horse. He lunged, grabbed, wrenched, and tumbled sideways as the rifle came free. As he did so, the gunman switched his aim, and again there was the sickening thump as a bullet smacked into the horse.

But McGill was down, prone, behind its bulk. The muzzle flashes had given away the bushwhacker's position. He now had Skinner's Spencer in his hands, seven slugs in the Blakeslee tube. Nevertheless, he was a long way from being out of the woods.

The sorrel had gone down thirty feet into the hollow from the narrow mouth of the arroyo, and dead centre. Getting back from there to the shelter of the rocky walls would be difficult. As the arroyo was left behind, the walls of Jackson's Hole fell away rapidly to left and right before swinging around and running parallel a couple of hundred feet apart. The sun was high, its fierce rays laying bare every crack or fissure, and about the only useful shelter McGill could see were hunks of deadwood under a stand of dying cottonwoods in the centre of the hollow, the fallen boulders up against both sides. Skinner and Devlin were behind those to his right, Harding to his left.

At that moment, McGill knew he was pinned down.

But, again, Harding had other ideas.

'Ewan!'

Jake Harding's roar, loud enough to send settling birds again soaring and wheeling.

'Yeah, Jake?'

'Cover me when I go in?'

A swashbuckling, never-say-die question in the voice. And McGill had just seven shots in the magazine, the only spare shells a long way out of his reach in Harding's saddle-bags.

But the bushwhackers wouldn't know that.

McGill twisted, came up on his side against the sorrel's warm belly, worked the Spencer's trigger guard and cocked the hammer.

'Go, Jake!'

As the words left his mouth he pushed himself up, lay prone across the horse and triggered his first shot. He saw it send chips of rock flying from the boulders, saw the flash of sunlight on a rifle barrel as a black-hatted individual hurriedly ducked back, caught the movement to his left as Harding broke cover and, Winchester in one hand, sprinted for the cottonwoods.

The black hat reappeared. A shot

rang out. But it was hurried and wasted as McGill's second aimed shot clipped the rock inches from the bushwhacker's head and again drove him back. And now Harding was into the trees, dust billowing as he hit the ground and rolled in amongst the deadwood with a crackle of snapping branches.

Then an eerie silence. The black specks of birds wheeling like waiting buzzards. Gunsmoke acrid in the hot air. Sweat trickling, breathing painfully tight, heart racing.

Five shots left — and nowhere to go.

Harding had made maybe thirty yards. He could go no further without sustained covering fire. If he did go again, he'd come up against two gunslingers behind cover — and McGill would almost certainly be out of shells before Harding reached the boulders.

The alternative was for McGill to make a move. But even with Harding laying down covering fire, there was only one place he could go. With the two of them in the cottonwoods, the advantage would have swung back to the bushwhackers.

McGill was still chewing his lip in a sweat of indecision when, with a squeal of pain, a glistening, wild-eyed horse exploded from the far side of the boulders and came hammering across the hardpan. The lean rider was flattened along the horse's straining neck, raking with his spur rowels hard enough to draw blood. Hooves thundered as he rode straight for the cottonwoods. Slugs from his blazing six-gun sent dead bark flying from the trees. Harding reared up, snapped one wild shot from the Winchester. Then the rider drove the horse crashing into the trees, and was on him. As McGill watched, he flung himself from the saddle. Both men went down in a tangle of limbs. Then one arm rose, a hand holding a six-gun slashed down. There was a sound like an axe biting into wood.

When McGill turned away, sickened,

the lean, black-garbed gunman he knew as Clete Skinner had advanced to within thirty feet of the dead sorrel and was grinning savagely at him along the barrel of a Winchester.

10

As Gord Brady rode away from Coyote Gulch with a shiny badge pinned under his vest, he was forced to admit that neither he nor his lawyer brother Mike had thought through their intentions. Ensuring that their niece, Verity Ketchum, was installed as the rightful, legal owner of Diamond K was a noble enough endeavour, but catching up with Jack Ketchum in Las Cruces, hanging on to his coat tail for almost 200 miles only to let him run loose in Coyote Gulch had been downright foolhardy.

All right, Brady knew he needn't accept the blame for Johnny McGill's death — maybe nobody could — but if he'd gone to the late Lew Drummond with his suspicions on the day he rode into town, well, maybe some things would have worked out differently.

Trouble was, at that time he *had* no reasonable suspicions. As far as anyone could tell, Jack Ketchum was a character who'd gone wild when his family broke up and — although still wanted in Mexico — was just as likely to settle down and become a respectable rancher when Diamond K dropped into his lap. He'd learned of his father's death, and ridden across Texas to Coyote Gulch. Looked at that way, he was simply the bearer of sad news.

Ike Garvey had seen him arrive and, according to Ed Thorpe, that was the last heard of him until he turned up at Spur, then rode off Blake Seeger's spread with Jeffers, Devlin and Skinner and four stolen horses. And it was entirely possible that all that had transpired in the three weeks between his riding through the Gulch and the reappearance at Spur had been orchestrated by his three sidekicks.

At the outset, they'd warned off Ewan McGill. When that didn't work, they burned down his small spread on

Cottonwood Creek and rode into town to shoot down his son. Ed Thorpe had suggested that Diamond K's location could make it the Texas equivalent of Hole in the Wall, the outlaw hideout up in North Wyoming. That would explain its attraction to Devlin and Skinner — but why would they go to the trouble of riding 200 miles to wipe out a family when, with a bunch of outlaws picked up for a couple of gold eagles apiece in New Mexico, they could have taken and held Diamond K by force?

And that question, Brady thought ruefully, brought him back squarely to his errant nephew, Jack Ketchum.

Already many miles away from the Gulch, around him the terrain was shimmering under the heat of the midday sun. Mostly flat, it was broken here and there by stands of parched trees, and in areas where the land could be considered high there were the usual dark scars of arroyos bitten into the slopes by winter run-offs and flash floods.

Shifting his bandanna to wipe the sweat from the back of his neck, Brady drew rein, cocked an ankle up on to the horn and rolled himself a smoke.

Yeah, his nephew!

Plain talking Ed Thorpe had little doubt Jack Ketchum was as guilty as hell. And as he pinned the deputy's tin badge on Brady's shirt, he'd suggested that sticking close to the owlhoot was not just a good idea, it was the only idea they had. The starting point for McGill and Harding, he told Brady, was the McGill buckboard. But if Ketchum, along with Devlin and Skinner, was using a Spur line cabin as base, then he, Thorpe, would bet his life on its being the one that lay to the north and west of the spread, a couple of miles beyond a twisting arroyo that emerged into a broad basin known as Jackson's Hole — and that being the case his new deputy could cut across country and save himself some time.

Which, Brady thought wryly as he squinted into the sun and idly watched the distant haze of dust that had caught his eye fifteen minutes earlier, was fine if you knew where you were going, but of little use when you didn't.

Spur was near as damnit on the Pecos. The line cabin was fifteen miles north, ten miles west. By his reckoning, he had to be close.

And if he was close, what did that dust suggest? There was no breeze. At this time of year a rider would leave a dust trace that would hang in the air, gently drifting, but taking a long while to disperse. So, McGill and Harding?

He was still squinting, smoking and cogitating, when the sounds reached his ears. The faint ticking of a beetle? A bird's beak, tapping on hard rock? Or a volley of shots, the crack of exploding gunpowder reduced by distance to something so faint it would have been smothered by the sound of his horse's hooves had he not stopped to roll that cigarette.

Brady's jaw tightened. His black-booted foot slipped from the horn, found its stirrup. He pinched out his quirly, flicked it into the coarse grass, and with a touch of the spurs set off towards the distant dust haze.

* * *

From the high ground, he gazed down with mounting horror as, in a scorching hot amphitheatre, a deadly drama unfolded.

Far below him, an arroyo was a funnel leading out of a broad basin that was a natural heat trap. At the mouth of that dark funnel, a horse lay dead. A man lay behind the horse. Sunlight glinted on his rifle.

As Brady dragged his Winchester from its boot, kicked out of his stirrups, hit the ground and wriggled on his belly up to the edge of the rimrock, his eye was caught by sudden movement. A rider exploded from rock cover on the far side of the basin and galloped headlong for a stand of dead cotton-woods. In those trees, another man reared up, tried a desperate snap-shot with a rifle.

The man behind the dead horse was watching.

But what he hadn't seen was the lean, black-clad figure that came walking out of the rocks and made straight for him.

Clete Skinner.

Brady jacked a shell into the breech, slammed the rifle into his shoulder, took aim. His foresight settled on Clete Skinner's chest, stayed there, moving with the man, matching his steady pace.

Out of the corner of his eye he saw the rider crash into the cottonwoods, heard the faint crackle of dead timber, saw the flash of a gun lifted high and brought down like a club.

Then Skinner had neared the downed horse. The man behind it rose to his feet. Ewan McGill, staring into the muzzle of a rifle in the hands of Clete Skinner. Staring death in the face.

With a soft grunt of supreme satisfaction, Gord Brady squeezed the trigger and sent a slug winging through the hot air to slam into the dust alongside Clete Skinner's boot.

★ ★ ★

As the dust spurted, the planes of Skinner's face tightened. When the distant rifle's crack reached his ears in faint waves of heat-distorted sound, his thin lips twitched with amusement.

The rifle remained rock steady, lined up on the bridge of McGill's nose.

'Drop it!'

The voice from the high ground was also thinned by distance, but clear and deadly in its purpose.

'And if I don't?' Skinner's answering yell came back off the walls in a rolling echo.

'The next shot takes your goddamn head off!'

Skinner laughed.

'So two men die. Friend, you think my trigger finger won't take up that last fraction of an inch and plant a bullet in McGill's skull?'

'Maybe it will. But if it does, you'll never have the satisfaction of knowing.'

And now Skinner's lips peeled back in a snarl of frustration.

'I'll say it again. Drop the rifle. Then back off!'

The air quivered into a tense silence.

'It's a long way down,' Clete Skinner said softly to McGill. 'If I do like he says, me and Devlin'll be gone before he gets here. So don't you go thinkin' this is over; don't you for one second think it's finished — you hear me?'

Another slug clipped Skinner's toe, and now his eyes flickered, the rifle jerked in his hands. With a soft curse, he stepped back, let the Winchester fall at his feet. As he did so, Ewan McGill came around the dead horse, brought up the Spencer, saw Skinner's eyes settle on it, recognize it, saw the sudden hatred in his black eyes.

'Better,' the voice yelled — and now McGill, in control of the situation, listened to that voice, tried to come up with a name, and remembered a bearded man who had also gone down to a slashing six-gun at another time, in another place. Gord Brady.

Clete Skinner saw the dawning of realization and said, 'Yeah, like I told Blade, I never did trust that feller.'

'But you'd better trust me,' McGill said, and he was startled by the sudden anger, the almost uncontrollable urge to squeeze the trigger and blow this man off the face of the earth. 'Believe this: you make a wrong move, and I'll kill you just like you killed my boy.' Then, dragging his gaze off the hated face he looked towards the high ground and roared, 'Brady! Move yourself. I'll hold 'em until you get down here.'

Up on the rimrock, an arm was lifted in acknowledgement. Seconds later they heard the rattle of hooves, swiftly fading as Brady pointed the horse south to swing around and come in through the narrow arroyo.

'You think you can do that?'

'Hold you?' McGill looked beyond Skinner, saw the other man, Devlin, ride out of the cottonwoods and canter towards them, and nodded. 'One way or another. Easiest way is to plug you and take you into town belly-down. You and your pard.'

Devlin was close. McGill flicked the barrel of the Spencer in his direction, shouted, 'Hold it right there!' and, as Devlin pulled up, backed his horse, shifted in the saddle so that his right hip with its holstered pistol was freed for action, he caught the sudden movement of Skinner's right hand and swiftly swung the rifle back to cover him.

The palms of his hands were slick with sweat.

On Clete Skinner's face there was a sly grin.

'I told you: when Brady gets down here, me and Devlin'll be gone.'

'Try it, and you're dead men.'

'Nah. I know that rifle. Needs loadin'

and cockin'. You plug me, you'll still be workin' that thing when Devlin drops you.'

'That's a chance I'll take.'

'I don't think so. Not if you want to see your wife alive.'

McGill's fists tightened on the rifle.

'Where is she?'

Again that wily grin. 'With her brother. Stretch Ketchum. He's sweet talkin' her. Thing is, if we don't turn up — just the two of us — he'll know there's trouble and that'll push him over the edge. He wants Verity on his side. But more than that, he's crazy to get his hands on Diamond K. First sign of trouble, he'll figure she ain't worth the bother, and then . . . '

Hoarsely, McGill said, 'So what are you offerin'?'

'We ride in like he expects, I can fix it she stays alive.'

'How?'

Skinner shook his head. 'You don't need to know. Let's just say me and Devlin had this figured, and a slight

change of plan won't make no difference.'

'You're talkin' in riddles.'

'But one way or another, we're ridin'
out of here.' This was Blade Devlin,
edging his horse closer, swinging out to
the flank so that he was on the
periphery of McGill's vision.

'How's it to be?' said Skinner. 'Easy
— or hard?'

McGill hesitated.

'That storekeeper's in a bad way over
in them cottonwoods,' Devlin said.
'Maybe I hit him too hard. Maybe he's
got a thin skull . . . '

Desperately, McGill listened for the
sound of a rider entering the confines
of the arroyo — but heard nothing. He
flicked a glance at Devlin, sidestepping
his horse; looked at the pistol hanging
low on Clete Skinner's thigh; thought
of Jack Ketchum, getting more nervous
with each minute that passed and there
was no sign of his three sidekicks. And
he remembered the scent of his wife's
hair, the colour of ripe corn, and

visualized it as it would be if it was streaked and matted with blood . . .

'Ride,' he said thickly.

'You sayin' — ?'

'Just get out of here!' McGill exploded.

And he watched Devlin wheel his horse about and start across the basin as Clete Skinner scooped up the Winchester and followed him at a jog to where his horse was tethered in the rocks. Moments later, the two outlaws had come together and were raising dust as they hammered towards the north edge of the basin and took their horses up the steep slope and over the crest.

The last McGill saw of them was a brilliant flash of steel as Clete Skinner looked back just the once to raise his rifle aloft in a signal that might have been triumph, might have been a promise, but in any case was lost on McGill.

For by then, with a sick dread in his heart, he had set off across the hollow for the cottonwoods.

11

They crowded into the tiny cabin, the lean man in black and his rawboned companion, bringing with them the dry taste of dust and the sour odour of stale sweat, their angular frames seeming to fill the cramped, cluttered space. And even as the door slammed open and they stomped in out of the blazing heat, Verity McGill felt as if a giant fist had slammed into her middle.

As she pulled away from Jack Ketchum, rubbing her bruised arms, disappointment at not seeing Ewan drained the strength from her legs. She wobbled. Another shaky step brought the back of her legs up against the edge of the cot, and she sat down, instinctively steadying herself with her hands on the mattress.

But still she couldn't understand what was happening. These were the men who had burned down her home, the men who had been with her in the rattling buckboard when Jack had come riding out of the woods to her rescue. Yet now he seemed unsurprised by their sudden appearance and, as he looked at the black garbed ruffian, his eyes were calculating.

'Where's Jeffers?'

Skinner flashed a glance at Verity, then dropped his hat on the table and sat down on the creaking chair by the window. 'At a place called Jackson's Hole. Lookin' after Ewan McGill.'

Ketchum's eyes narrowed. 'So what the hell went wrong in town? Lew Drummond was already taken care of, his deputy no more use than — '

'Easy now,' Skinner cut in, and he raised a cautionary hand and again looked across the room at Verity. 'It's a long story, but let's say when things got straightened out I figured that gal there might have strong objections to your plans — so I grabbed us some insurance.'

'What about the other half of the job?'

'All took care of.'

'What does he mean?' Verity's voice trembled as she looked at her brother. 'How do you know these men? And what's taken care of?'

Skinner scowled as Ketchum hesitated with obvious discomfiture. 'Ma'am, your brother there, he decided it was best to get everybody likely to inherit Diamond K out of the way, permanent. The reason he rode down here, you know?'

'No,' she said. 'I don't know. He came here to tell me about my father, to ask me to . . . to sign some papers. And what do you mean, out of the way? If you've got Ewan, what's happened to my son, Johnny?'

'Your boy's dead,' Skinner said, and at that flat statement, spoken by a man no longer bothering to hide the gleam of amusement in his black eyes, Verity rocked backwards and moaned softly.

'You goddamn fool!' Ketchum said.

'Hell, listen who's mouthin' off,' Skinner said scornfully, and Blade Devlin shook his head, stepped across the dirt floor, swung around to plant a haunch on the cold iron stove.

'You're the fool, Stretch. Your way'd never work — '

'The hell it wouldn't! And what now? You think she'll sign those papers knowin' her boy's dead?'

'Never!' Verity said brokenly. Her face was ashen, her eyes glistening with unshed tears.

'Why, that's exactly what she will do,' Clete Skinner said. 'She rides — '

'I told you, I won't do it!'

'She rides to Hancock, signs them papers,' Skinner went on remorselessly, 'she gets her husband back alive and well. If she don't . . . '

The unfinished threat hung in the air. A sob caught in Verity's throat and she brought her clenched fist to her mouth, bit hard on the knuckles, praying for the pain to overwhelm her grief.

Johnny dead. Ewan held by a man

called Jeffers. She remembered him, a stocky man with a shotgun. At the house, he had poured the coal oil. Devlin had struck the match. And Skinner . . . Skinner had stood back, holding her easily — and laughing.

'How . . . how do I know you'll let him go?'

'You don't — '

'My word on it,' Ketchum interrupted, glaring at Skinner.

Verity laughed. 'The word of a killer.'

'Not me.' Ketchum shook his head.

'But your idea, your filthy scheme,' Verity said and, as she met and held her brother's eyes, stared into his soul, he was the one to drop his gaze and look away.

'Never mind.' She shook her head, clamped her trembling hands between her thighs, gazed with contempt at the three men. 'I'll do it: I have to. I'll ride with you to Fort Hancock and I'll sign those papers. The ranch will be yours. But before I do anything, I must see Ewan. I must know he's alive

— otherwise, there's no point in any of this.'

'No time,' Skinner said flatly.

'But — '

'Yes or no?' Devlin said.

'Oh, goddamn every one of you!' Verity said, and when she bent her head, hot tears fell like rain on to her clenched fists.

Part Three

THE PURSUIT

12

'Jake, I hate to say this, but there's no way you can go on.'

'Thickest skull in Coyote Gulch,' Jake Harding grumbled, 'and that's the way I acted, lettin' that danged owlhoot get the jump on me.'

'Thick or not, you're concussed and that means you stay right here.'

'Hell, you're just sayin' that so you can take my horse.'

He was sitting slumped forward on a boulder in the scant shade of the cottonwoods, elbows on spread knees, powerful hands dangling from limp wrists. His Stetson had absorbed some of the slashing blow's killing power, but drying blood glistened in the storekeeper's iron-grey hair, and his weatherbeaten face was pale and glistening.

'McGill's right,' said Gord Brady.

'And from the way those fellers lit out, I'd say we need to hurry.'

He'd burst from the arroyo into Jackson's Hole in time to see the plume of dust dispersing into a haze over the far ridge, and had cantered across to where Ewan McGill was helping Harding get comfortable. McGill had caught the glint of the tin badge as Brady dismounted, and mentally congratulated Ed Tranter on his new post and for his fast thinking in at once swearing in a deputy and dispatching him in the right direction.

'Yeah, I know it,' Harding admitted, 'and I'd only hold you back. You reckon they're at that cabin?'

'Where else?' said Brady. 'They headed north and, by my reckoning, Ketchum can't be more than two or three miles away.'

'But not for too long,' said McGill. 'What they had figured for a smooth ride's turned into a nightmare. They'll give Ketchum the good news then hit the trail for Hancock.'

'And take Verity along?'

'Jake, your guess is as good as mine.'

'You can bet on it,' Brady said grimly. 'They need her to keep you at arm's length.'

'Holdin' her,' McGill argued, 'ensures I'll stick to 'em like a burr to a blanket. And she'll slow them down. They don't want that. Much easier to leave her behind.'

Brady shook his head. 'I don't believe they'll do that.'

'No,' McGill said, and felt sick to his stomach. 'And I'd be a fool to believe Ketchum'll keep her alive when she's no more use.'

'Two on three,' Harding said, gingerly touching his scalp. 'Fair odds, and if you move fast and jump them — '

'Let's go!'

In less than five minutes they had Harding comfortable in the shade behind the tumbled boulders, two full canteens and Brady's Winchester at his side. Then, after a brief, firm handshake, McGill swung aboard Harding's horse and followed Gord Brady to the far ridge.

He had Clete Skinner's Spencer in his saddle boot, two cartons of shells in the saddle-bags, the storekeeper's Colt at his hip. The first skirmish had been won. Whichever way you looked at it, Skinner and Devlin were on the run. And in his heart, for the first time since he had ridden away from the charred embers of his home, there was hope in his heart.

He was riding after Verity.

* * *

Beyond the basin known as Jackson's Hole the terrain became uneven and more wooded, the indistinct trail twisting its way through low hills whose flanks were blanketed with trees. Like the arroyo, this was drygulch country. But both McGill and Brady were convinced that Skinner and Devlin had pouched their weapons and were now intent on rejoining Ketchum.

'Killin' you don't make good sense now the law's on to them,' Brady said, as they rode along the side of a thickly wooded slope and McGill's scalp crawled as he eyed the impenetrable trees.

'All they know,' he pointed out, 'is a feller they rode with was up on the rimrock in a position to drill them full of holes.'

'And too far away to flash a badge,' Brady conceded.

'Skinner allowed he never trusted you.'

'The whole ride down from Las Cruces we were eyein' each other like mistrustful dogs.'

'And now you're on his tail.'

'So who needs a badge?' Brady said, grinning. 'With you and me after 'em they'll cut and run for Hancock and Diamond K, take their chance on gettin' their hands on them deeds.'

There were clear signs of the two outlaws' passing. White wood glistened in the dappled sunlight where branches had been jaggedly snapped. Sharp hooves had cut into the softer earth, scarring the grass darkly. And once, when they emerged into the open and lowered their heads so that hat brims shaded their eyes from the sudden, dazzling glare, they could see down a gentle slope and across level ground to the trees a thousand yards ahead and there, for an instant, something moved and was gone. So fleeting was the impression of movement that it could have been a trick of the light — but McGill was convinced.

'That's them,' he said. 'And now we're that close, we take extra care.'

'With Harding downed, I doubt they'll be expecting us so soon.'

'Then we keep them in the dark until it's too late.'

Brady chuckled. 'For a feller running a handful of cows on a muddy creek you'd make a pretty fair regulator.'

'A man learns fast when killers come gunnin' for his family.' He cast a sideways glance at Brady and said,

'That explains my motives, but what brings you into this? When we talked in the saloon, Ed Tranter couldn't figure which camp you were in. The next time I see you, he's pinned a badge on your vest.'

'My second story must have rung true.' The big man shrugged, a thoughtful expression softening the scarred, bearded face. 'For a while I was Diamond K ramrod. I moved out when I saw Earl J. was dealin' from a stacked deck. I'd hate to see Stretch Ketchum take it down the same crooked road.'

They crossed the softer level ground and approached the trees and, as their horses kicked up clods of earth, McGill knew he had not been wrong. They were treading in the fresh tracks of two horses that had passed that way, and had themselves followed others. Ketchum and Verity had led the way. Skinner and Devlin could be no more than three-quarters of a mile ahead and, by his reckoning, that put them very close to the cabin.

'Spur land lies to the east,' McGill said, as they pointed their horses up a sharp rise and urged them through tangled brush already broken by the owlhoots. 'This woodland don't extend in that direction. The cabin's most likely on the eastern fringe of the trees, a fine spot to overlook Seeger's open range.'

'A spring for fresh water, maybe a rope corral, windows and door on the front wall.' Brady nodded, squinted ahead. 'We'll be on them before those two have had time to wash the dust out of their throats and put Ketchum wise. But trappin' them in the cabin ain't such a good idea.'

'If they hold a pistol to Verity's head, we're done for,' McGill agreed flatly.

'But if there's woods behind the cabin like you say, we'll be in a position to pick them off as they ride off.'

'In cold blood?'

'Isn't that what they've done once,

and tried a second time?'

McGill's eyes were bleak. 'You're right.' Leather creaked as he twisted to reach into a saddle bag. He took out the box of Spencer ammunition, broke it open, stuffed shells into his pockets. Then, as he leaned down to ease the rifle in its boot, the sound of raised voices was carried to them on the warm breeze.

'Closer than I thought.'

Brady nodded. His rifle was resting across his thighs.

'I don't know if I can go through with this.'

'I can tell them I'm law,' Brady said, 'if that'll make you feel better. *Then* we shoot them.'

The woods thinned. Over a long, naked hump rising from a bed of tangled weeds, they could see the sun beating down on a roof of rotting shingles, a blackened tin chimney poking through. Cautiously, they skirted the bare hillock, staying back in the trees. The voices became clearer. A horse snorted. A metal shoe rang on stone.

Then they were close enough to see the gradient on the east side of the hump that descended from dappled shade into clear sunlight. They were looking at the rear and side of the old log cabin that had been built in a small clearing hacked out of the earth. Bounded on the west by the woods, Seeger's Spur range stretched away in three directions and, at this point, they were high enough to see the distant golden gleam of the Pecos.

Two horses were standing on the hard-packed earth in front of the cabin. As McGill watched, Devlin came into view and swung into the saddle. He was followed by the black-clad Skinner who also mounted up, wheeled his horse on tight reins and called angrily to someone hidden by the cabin.

The answer was indistinct. Seconds later, the hidden rider was revealed as he moved away from the cabin, cutting across Skinner and Devlin before putting the open range at his back and pointing his horse towards the slope. He was holding a lead rope that was dallied around the horn. The other end was attached to McGill's mare.

'Verity,' McGill said huskily.

She was riding bareback, head lifted proudly, fair hair gleaming in the bright sunshine, doing nothing to urge the mare forwards; doing nothing at all to help her brother.

'Back off,' Brady said sharply.

Clenching his teeth, sawing on the reins, McGill walked the reluctant horse backwards into the trees, out of the corner of his eye saw Brady doing the same while struggling to keep the rifle lifted and ready. Fifty feet away, Ketchum raked his spurs and sent his mount lunging up the slope and on through the weeds towards the naked hump. The mare whinnied as the lead rope snapped tight. Then it, too, was attacking the incline in awkward, jerky bounds, hooves slipping and sliding as the rope threatened to drag it off balance, Verity rocking backwards and clinging tight to the rough halter.

Skinner and Devlin were hanging back, watching, arguing.

But once they moved, Verity would be trapped in the middle: Ketchum in front, the two gunmen close behind.

Face tight, McGill reached down into his boot, came up holding a knife and glanced through the trees at Brady. The big man caught the glint of steel, nodded his understanding and swung to face the cabin and the two outlaws who had now quit talking and begun to move.

With a grunt, McGill clamped the blade of the knife between his teeth and dug in his heels to send his horse bounding out of the trees. He swung right, careered hard across the slope, heard Skinner's yell, squinted ahead to see Ketchum still blind to what was going on as he fought to keep the reluctant mare moving.

A shot rang out. Verity's head flashed around and she saw McGill. And now, as McGill thundered down on them, Ketchum became aware that something was wrong. There was a snarl on his lean face as he swung in the saddle. And, closing fast, McGill looked across and met pale eyes that were devoid of normal human feelings.

Then he was on them, as Brady's Winchester roared and pistol fire rattled. Ignoring the snick of bullets through the branches, he slammed up against the mare's flank, snatched the knife from his teeth and leaned down to part the taut rope with a single sweeping slash. The sudden release of tension rocked Ketchum's horse. Still facing the wrong way, the outlaw toppled sideways, the hand that had been reaching for his pistol now grabbing for the horn.

'Ride, Verity!' McGill roared. With his left hand, he grabbed the mare's halter. Already swinging his own mount in a flurry of thrashing hooves and flying mane, he saw his wife kick hard with her heels. As he turned away the mare came with him, teeth bared, so close that there was a crushing pressure on his leg, first keeping pace then swiftly surging ahead and tearing the halter from his hand as Verity reached out to touch him, eyes alight as she laughed out loud with excitement.

Skinner and Devlin were snapping shots from the shelter of the cabin, pinned down by Brady's accurate rifle fire. Still pulling away, Verity took in the situation at a glance, cut behind the big man and sent the mare crashing deep into the trees.

McGill let her go.

A pistol cracked behind him. The slug slammed into a tree, showering him with bark. Then he had tumbled from the saddle and was reaching for the big Spencer. As he pulled it free, a glance behind told him that Ketchum was still in the saddle, snapping wild shots as he struggling to bring his horse around. McGill dropped to one knee, fired once with the Spencer, took the comforting kick in the shoulder as the big slug zipped through the lean man's shirt and drew a roar of anger.

That close call drove home the truth: occupying the higher ground, protected by the trees, McGill and Brady held all the aces. With a blood-curdling Rebel yell, Ketchum blasted a final defiant shot in McGill's direction then wrenched his horse cruelly about and sent it galloping back down the slope.

'Let's ride!' he yelled and, as he tore across the front of the cabin and disappeared from sight, the two outlaws pulled back. Seconds later, there came the rattle of hooves. Brady burst from the trees, ran across at an angle behind the cabin in a vain attempt to keep the three men in sight. He was too late. Rapidly, the beat of hooves faded.

'Leave them be,' McGill said.

Then there was the crackle of brush behind him, the sound of breath catching in a throat and, when Brady tramped back, Ewan McGill was holding his sobbing wife in his hands, his face buried in her hair.

13

They pulled off the rough trail when they had flogged their horses unmercifully with quirt and spur for close on an hour through the scorching heat, stopping only when Skinner yelled ahead to Ketchum and pointed to where the land dipped to a hollow in which rank water had collected around the twisted roots of a stand of cottonwoods. There, the three dust-caked men flung themselves from the saddle, ground-tethered their blowing, head-hung mounts, and limped stiffly into what little shade they could find under the thin canopy of grey-green leaves.

Ketchum was drenched in sweat, and throughout the ride had been thumping the saddle horn in frustration and throwing black looks at his sidekicks.

Skinner was unfazed. Each time

Ketchum's furious gaze swung his way he grinned wolfishly; each time the enraged outlaw faced front he looked owlishly across at Devlin. It was a joke shared: Ketchum had blown it. Getting his hands on Diamond K had always been a risk, but without his sister that risk was doubly dangerous.

'Goddamn you, Clete, you lied,' Ketchum gritted through clenched teeth. 'That, or McGill somehow got away from Jeffers.' He glowered at Skinner. 'You think he could do that — or what?'

Skinner, now hunkered down rolling a smoke, shrugged. 'You'd better know now, Jeffers is dead. Back in the Gulch, that storekeeper give him a face full of buckshot.' He finished the cigarette, scraped a match on his boot, blew a stream of smoke. 'But what I did would have worked. That gal would've done every damn thing you asked of her if McGill hadn't shown up.'

'And now she won't, because we ain't got her and she knows her man's safe.

Now they'll come after us, hound us all the way to Hancock.'

Devlin spat. 'Who? That storekeeper's nursing a cracked skull back in Jackson's Hole. Why would he take the trouble? And, like you say, McGill's back with his wife. You think he'll be spoilin' for a fight?'

'What I think,' Ketchum said, 'is he's out to get the man killed his boy.'

'Let him try,' Skinner said, and laughed.

'He will,' Ketchum said, 'and seein' as you're ridin' along with me, that could put him close enough to make my claim on Diamond K look like so much horseshit.'

'The hell with it,' said Devlin. 'The idea of turnin' that spread into some kind of robbers' roost was horseshit anyhow. You ain't no Jesse James, Stretch. Ain't no band of owlhoots gonna line up behind you, rob trains, banks — '

'You turnin' down the chance of a spread worth thousands anyway? You tellin' me I should walk away from an inheritance just because some feller runnin' a few cows on a muddy creek bears a grudge?'

'Grudge,' Devlin echoed, and sniggered. 'Clete damn near cut his son in two pieces, Stretch.'

'McGill comes after me,' Ketchum said, 'he gets the same.'

'Him and big Gord Brady,' Devlin pointed out.

'Ah, yeah,' Ketchum breathed, his eyes suddenly narrow with speculation. 'That feller was Diamond K ramrod, right? His brother's the lawyer holdin' them deeds over there in Hancock. Maybe he's got plans of his own. Maybe Mike Brady's fixed things so brother Gord gets the spread, all legal like.'

Skinner sucked hard on the cigarette, his black eyes ugly.

'So how do we play it?'

'Huh?'

'Dry-gulchin' ain't worked. We could try again — but maybe they'll split up.

161

They do that, we'll be settin' in the woods waitin' for something to point a gun at, they'll be halfway to Hancock.'

'Jesus!' Ketchum said. 'They could do that, if they're smart. And all they need do is warn that lawyer — '

'If your sister rides with them,' Skinner said, 'there ain't no warnin' needed 'cause you can kiss that spread goodbye.'

'So here's how we play it,' Ketchum said. He sprang up, paced impatiently. 'We rode for nigh on an hour. I'd say that puts us *more* than an hour ahead because they'll have plenty of talkin' to do.'

Skinner nodded. 'And your sis'll figure even if you get to Hancock before her, ain't no way you can get your hands on the spread because she's the legal heir.'

'So what we do is use every second of that hour we've got,' Ketchum said, 'and make damn sure we do get there before her.'

'And then?'

Something unpleasant flickered behind Jack Ketchum's eyes, and even the hardened Skinner was forced to look away. He disguised the movement by flicking away the quirly as he climbed to his feet, glanced once at Devlin and almost imperceptibly shook his head.

'Then,' Ketchum said, his gaze turned to the heat haze shimmering over the distant heights of the Diablo Plateau, 'we step into a certain office and have us a friendly talk with a lawyer name of Mike Brady.'

★ ★ ★

To Ewan McGill, his wife's fortitude was unbelievable. After that first, emotional reunion he had been summoning up the courage to break the news of Johnny's death when she looked him in the eye, reached up to his lips and silenced him with the lightest touch of a finger.

'Ewan, I already know,' she said. 'That terrible man Skinner . . . '

At that point, though her spirit was indomitable, her voice had broken; at that point, too, Gord Brady — briefly introduced — had left them to their shared grief and had not approached them again until the rich aroma of fresh-brewed coffee was drifting from the open door of the cabin.

And that, McGill reckoned, had been close on an hour ago.

'It's about time,' he said, from the table by the window, 'we decided what we're goin' to do.'

'We go after them,' Brady said bluntly. 'They killed your boy, now they intend to steal Diamond K.'

'You're a lawman,' Verity said, acknowledging his duty, 'but there are three of them. You don't stand a chance.'

Brady shook his head. 'Maybe. But I'm more than a lawman. I guess time and distance got in the way of the two of us ever meetin', but I'm your ma's brother, and until a year ago, I was your pa's foreman. That gives me a vested interest in Diamond K, and a strong incentive to go after the man who killed my . . . ?' His grin was tinged with sadness. 'If I'm your uncle, what would that've made me to young Johnny?'

'Goodness!' Verity said. She sat down on the edge of the cot, her cheeks pink. 'Great uncle, or something like that, I suppose.' Then she frowned. 'If you do go after them, Gord, what about poor Jake Harding down there in Jackson's Hole?'

'Jake'll survive because you'll go pick him up, take him into town,' McGill said.

'And what about you?'

'I've a score to settle: I ride with Brady.'

'And haven't I got some business to take care of?'

He frowned. 'Diamond K?'

'Come on, Ewan! A big spread's something we always wanted. Now both my parents are dead, Diamond K's ours.' Her lips quivered as she smiled. 'We must do it, for Johnny's sake. All we have to do is ride to Hancock and identify ourselves.'

'That's the easy bit,' Brady said, 'as you'll see when you get there. The lawyer who's handled Diamond K's affairs for the past five years is my brother, Mike.'

McGill's eyes narrowed. 'Sounds to me like meeting those owlhoots in Las Cruces was no happenstance.'

'And you'd be right. No time to tell it now, but Ed Thorpe's got the full story, which is why I'm wearin' a badge. And that brings us to the hard bit: sure, my brother's the lawyer you need to see, but Jack Ketchum's got a head start on you, and when he gets to Hancock he ain't likely to take Mike's no for an answer.'

'Ewan?'

McGill looked into Verity's eyes, saw the puffiness there caused by hot tears she had courageously brushed aside, saw the new light in them that was bright enough to banish grief — for a while — and told him she was prepared to reach out to take what was hers if only he would go with her. And he sighed, because some miles ahead there were three dusty, armed men pushing tired horses towards the same goal, and if it came to a showdown in the streets of Fort Hancock, it would be no place for a woman.

'Min Harding's been handling the . . . been doin' what has to be done,' he said softly. 'She arranged Johnny's funeral for this morning. We couldn't be there, so I reckon the least we can do for him is show some guts, go get the bastard who killed him — and then, in time, maybe we'll plant a rose at Diamond K, name it after the boy we lost.'

'I'll need one of those old saddles,' Verity said huskily, 'or I'll be too sore to make that ride. But that's all I need because, with you two fellers alongside me, I know I can't fail.' She grinned, and now her eyes were shining through unspilled tears. 'Come on, Ewan McGill, let's show this greenhorn lawman how we ride to Hancock.'

14

They rode out in the blistering heat of early afternoon, pushing on hard with the dust coating their slick skin and their eyes squinting into the glittering orb of the sun that had now slid past the meridian and was beginning its long journey to the far western horizon.

They pushed their mounts hard, but without recklessness. A good horse will comfortably cover twelve miles in each hour, and with Gord Brady's estimate of the distance that lay ahead of them at some 120 miles, that suggested they need only hold their pace to be in Hancock by eight that evening.

But as they pushed on towards Sierra Blanca the terrain they must ride over would become increasingly severe, they were not riders of the legendary Pony Express, and they could not benefit from a change of horses at regular intervals. The fittest of cow ponies could not hold even that moderate pace indefinitely, so out of necessity they drew rein and rested after the first hour; rested again an hour later; and because each rest period lasted ten minutes while riders and horses gathered breath and slaked their thirst — when that was possible — natural instinct and a burning impatience told them that each stop put them that much further behind their quarry.

Logic told them that their instincts were wrong.

Jack Ketchum and his cronies were in the unenviable position of being out in front with their heads forever twisted to watch their back-trail. Their instincts — the instincts of the hunted — would convince them that the pursuers were gaining ground. Buried deep in their minds, logic and common sense would strive to warn them that they must slow down, but the fear that tormented them, gripped their innards like cold cramps and forced them again and again to rake their flagging horses with the cruel rowels of their spurs, would refuse to listen.

Yes, they would pull ahead; but the headlong charge towards Hancock that might last one hour, two hours, miraculously stretch even to three or four hours at the same demented pace, would inevitably slow. And when it slowed, that slowdown would be dramatic.

That knowledge kept the chasing group in good heart.

'You wait and see,' Gord Brady said hoarsely into the choking dust, 'they'll come back to us like a steer hittin' the end of a dallied lass-rope.'

He spoke over his shoulder as they cantered through a glade of trees, forced into single file where the trail snaked through deceptive, dappled sunlight, and even as those cheerful, sanguine words left his mouth he was abruptly swept from the saddle like a child's rag doll, his startled yell snapped off as his big frame was dumped on the trail and all the breath was driven from his body.

Close behind him, Ewan McGill hauled his horse to a stiff-legged sliding halt that left it sitting on its haunches, at the same time twisting in the saddle to yell a warning to Verity.

When his horse scrambled to its feet and McGill faced front, his sweating throat was inches from the rope, still ominously humming, that hard, calloused hands had pulled taut and lashed to a tree on either side of the trail.

★　★　★

Thirty miles after they had rigged the rope across the trail, Blade Devlin's horse, flanks streaming white lather and stumbling with the helplessness of an animal ridden to the brink of death, stepped in a gopher hole and snapped its right foreleg.

Clete Skinner blew smoke from the

muzzle of his .45 as the echoes of the shot that had put the horse out of its agony died away, and turned to shake his head at Jack Ketchum.

'Ridin' double ain't no option,' he said, looking to where the man who had come tumbling from the saddle was slumped on a boulder with a glazed look in his eyes and blood dripping from a smashed nose.

'You're right; Devlin stays,' Ketchum agreed, and grinned wolfishly. 'Maybe that clumsy nag's done us a good turn. I'll breathe easier with someone else watchin' my back-trail.'

'I'll hold them,' Devlin mumbled, looking on numbly as Skinner swung down, crossed to the dead horse and dragged the Winchester from under its body.

'No, you'll kill them,' Ketchum said. 'Make sure you get them off my back, permanent. No fancy warnings, no chances taken. Let 'em come close enough so you can't miss, then blow 'em out of the saddle.'

'They'll see the horse, know something's wrong.'

'Not if you move back down the trail a-ways.'

'And the girl?'

Ketchum shrugged as if the matter was of complete indifference. 'With fast shootin' you can take McGill and Brady. If she's fool enough to hang around with them two dead . . . '

Skinner tossed the Winchester. Devlin caught it, smearing the bright metal with his bloody hands, came up off the rock. Ketchum looked back once after he'd kicked his weary horse into motion and ridden a fast fifty yards. Blade Devlin had climbed the bank and was walking away along the edge of the thick woods. Fifty yards beyond him, the trail swept right. Once round that bend, he would melt into the trees.

Two shots, Ketchum thought with satisfaction. They were riding into the sun, Devlin shooting from cover; just two shots would put paid to McGill and Brady. And if Verity thought about his offer, decided to come all the way to Hancock, she'd have no choice but to dance to his tune.

He was whistling thinly through his teeth when Clete Skinner caught up, and the light in his eyes was the light of a man seeing the fulfilment of his dreams.

* * *

The healing wound on Gord Brady's cheek had been split open as he slammed face down on the hard trail, and wet blood was a bright sheen seeping through the curling hairs of his dark beard as he climbed shakily to his feet.

McGill came cantering back down the trail leading the lawman's runaway horse as Verity slid from the saddle and ran across to take the big man's arm. He stumbled, his eyes glassy, then shook his leonine head and gently eased himself out of her grip.

'Where'd it catch you?'

He grinned sheepishly at McGill, took the proffered reins, dragged the back of his hand across his face and grimaced at the red stain.

'Missed my fool neck, or I'd be a gonner. Damn idiots strung it too low.'

'You're a big man, on a big horse,' McGill said. 'If it had been Verity out in front . . .'

'But it wasn't,' she said firmly, 'and that's one trap we won't fall into a second time.'

Brady walked his horse off the trail, hunkered down under the trees, began rolling a cigarette.

'It'll get harder. Sun's sinkin'. 'Fore long it'll be in our eyes. With high ground ahead they'll maybe have us in their sights.'

'When they followed me and Johnny into the Gulch,' McGill said, 'they watched us through glasses.' He dug his canteen out of his saddle-bag, handed it down to Verity, his face troubled. 'There's still time . . .'

'No,' she said, reading his mind. 'I'll not go back because this trouble is Diamond K trouble, and that makes it mine, not yours. And how do you know they're watching us? As far as they know, once I'd been rescued you backed off, gave it up as a bad job and rode back to see Ed Thorpe in the Gulch.'

'Then why the rope?'

'A precaution. They don't *know*, but there will be doubts.'

'On both sides,' McGill said. 'We're ridin' in the dark, and if you were to take a bullet — '

'That rope was put there to slow us down — if we're following them — not kill us,' she cut in firmly.

'And it worked. But Brady's right, what if they are watching, and start shooting?'

'You're not thinking, Ewan. To shoot us, they have to stop, set up an ambush. If they take time to do that, they've given away their precious lead.' She looked into his eyes, shook the canteen, listened to the thin slosh of water then dribbled some into her palm and held it up to dampen her horse's mouth.

Brady chuckled out a thin billow of smoke. 'She's right.'

'We can't be sure.'

'Hell, no, this whole business has been guesswork from the start. Maybe they've had a bellyful of trouble. Makin' for Hancock's the same as makin' for the border. Maybe they'll ride straight on through town, cross the Bravo, take up where they left off in Las Cruces.'

'And maybe they won't. Verity, you've been closest to Ketchum, looked into his eyes: d'you think he'll give up, ride away from Diamond K?'

'No matter what I think we can't back away now,' Verity said softly. 'There's so much to gain. I understand your concern for me, but if I turn around and ride away from here I'm on my own, with you I'm safe — aren't I?'

'He can't guarantee it,' Gord Brady said. 'Nobody can.' He came up off the ground in a rangy movement that belied his bulk, flicked away the cigarette, stretched to his full, impressive height. 'That bein' the case, we've got to choose between them two options — but we've got to make that decision in a hurry.'

'I say stay behind,' McGill said to Verity, easing his weight in the saddle, watching her toy with the empty canteen. 'Jake's laid up in Jackson's Hole. You could make it back to the cabin in an hour or so, get fresh water, be at the Hole soon after. That way you'll help Jake, put my mind at rest.'

'And lose Diamond K if Jack beats you?'

'Dammit!' McGill said fiercely, 'your bein' there won't change a thing if he's that good.'

'Both of you'll lose it anyway,' Brady said, 'if we toss this back and forth much longer.'

'Then that settles it, and there's absolutely nothing you can do,' Verity said sweetly and, despite his chagrin, McGill found himself suppressing a smile. 'When you turn around and head for Hancock, I'll be right behind you.'

'Then make damn sure you stay there,' McGill growled, and with a shake of the head he wheeled his horse and set off down the trail.

Verity flashed Brady a quick smile, felt herself flush as he winked broadly, let him mount up and follow McGill, then swung into the saddle.

They rode that way for an hour, the trail gradually steepening as it wound its way into the Singing Hills. And it was the winding nature of the trail and the woods lying thick on either side that for some time prevented them from seeing the circling buzzards.

It was Verity who spotted them, and yelled a warning — but by then it was too late.

15

Blade Devlin played it cagey, letting two of the horses clatter by beneath him before slipping silently out of the woods on to a grassy bank ten feet above the trail with his Winchester levelled.

McGill was already a hundred yards away, Brady some fifty yards back. Still riding easily at the rear — because trouble, surely, would come from somewhere ahead — and looking idly beyond the two men at the beauty of the reddening skies, Verity picked out the lazily wheeling specks, recognized them with a shudder of revulsion and called out.

The metallic, oily click from behind and above was unmistakable. She gasped, and whirled in the saddle. Devlin's unshaven face was split by a savage grin. The muzzle of the rifle was lined up on her back and so unexpectedly close that she jerked with shock, then froze. Misinterpreting the movement, her horse tossed its head and obediently drew to a halt.

'Stay like that,' Devlin said — and edged closer; so close as he eased down the steep shelf of the bank that the warm steel of the Winchester's muzzle brushed against her shirt then pressed hard against her spine.

'Verity?'

More than fifty yards away now, Brady turned to look back. As he did so, his vest pulled to one side. The late afternoon light glinted on his deputy's badge. Behind Verity, Blade Devlin caught that sudden gleam. He uttered a low, startled oath, and the rifle probed with renewed viciousness.

It seemed that, for an instant, Gord Brady saw the girl, and nothing more; a slight kink in the trail put Devlin behind her so that he was hidden by the bulk of horse and rider.

Then, restless, sharply alert to the smell of sweat and fear, Verity's horse snorted and took two steps sideways across the trail.

It was enough. Blade Devlin was exposed.

'McGill, they're behind us!' Brady roared out the warning as his right hand slapped leather. Up ahead, Ewan McGill snatched a quick glance backwards, then spun his horse on a dime and started back.

'Leave it!' Devlin yelled at Brady, and flipped the rifle sideways to blast a single shot over the lawman's head. At the same time he came off the bank in a leap that carried him on to Verity's horse. The nervous animal again jinked sideways. Devlin swayed, regained his balance, then his hard body pressed tight up against Verity's stiff back. With a sudden, startled gasp, she felt his sinewy arm come over her shoulder and clamp like a bar of iron across her throat.

* * *

The second shot clipped a twig above McGill's head. The muzzle flash was bright under the trees, and came from a position frighteningly close to Verity. Unable to see just where or who the man was, McGill drove his horse on, instinctively dipping for his six-gun, cocking it as it slid smoothly out of its holster.

Then he was bearing down on Brady and his eyes widened in shock as the lawman quickly swung his horse across the trail, teeth bared in a snarl of impotent rage, stiff arm lifted to bar the way — and again McGill found himself clenching his teeth as he wrenched his horse out of its headlong gallop on tight reins, spinning it hard as dust spurted and billowed and above the snort of horses and the creak of leather and the rattle of flying stones that all but drowned Brady's barked words another voice was raised in mocking laughter.

'It's Devlin!' Brady called again, his voice loud and bitter with self-recrimination. 'I think he's alone — but he's got Verity.'

'Jesus!'

Side on, cocked pistol in his uplifted hand and standing loose-legged in the stirrups as his excited horse danced skittishly under him, McGill looked down the trail and saw his wife sitting stiffly upright in the saddle with the Winchester tight up against her body, the muscular arm across her throat, the man's Stetson — and little else; no part of his body presented a target.

'Stay put!' Devlin roared.

'All right, all right,' McGill called, sweating. 'We ain't moving, take it easy, feller.'

'Devlin,' Brady said, 'as a lawman I'm telling you to let the woman go, and you can ride out of here.'

'She stays with me.'

'Then you won't get away with it.'

'Not played this way. I turn and ride away, I get a bullet in the back.'

'Right. So we've got a stand-off.'

'No. You ride — '

He broke off, uttering an oath as Verity suddenly wriggled, arched her back and slid her head out from under his arm. Her flailing arm knocked the Winchester aside. She flung a leg forwards across the horse's neck, rolled sideways . . .

Fifty yards up the trail, McGill kicked his horse with his heels and sent it surging forwards. Gord Brady edged his horse to the side, staying back but giving himself a clear line of fire.

. . . And Devlin caught Verity's shirt collar with his left hand, yanked her backwards, then rammed her down and held her half on and half off the horse, her face pressed into the long mane.

'All right, enough!' Devlin yelled, swinging the Winchester — and McGill hauled rein, slid to a halt; waited.

'Now you do like I say.' Devlin was panting, concentrating on holding the woman, on keeping the Winchester level while controlling the horse with his knees. 'You turn around, and you ride away. You keep goin', and you don't look back.'

'And Verity?' McGill said hoarsely.

'She's in my goddamn way — but I don't let her loose until you're so far down that trail there ain't no way back. You figure I'm wrong, decide on a rush — the woman gets it in — '

And again he broke off, snarling, as Verity renewed her desperate struggle. She drove her elbow back like a piston. It rammed into Devlin's soft underbelly. He gasped, started to bend at the waist. As he did so, Verity continued the violent backward motion, straightening and lifting her arm. The back of her hand cracked across his nose. Devlin bellowed. His roar of pain startled the horse. It squealed and reared. Sitting awkwardly behind the cantle, Devlin began to slide backwards. He had too much to do, and not enough hands. With a lithe wriggle, Verity flung herself away from the horse and landed lightly on her feet.

'Now!' Brady roared.

But McGill was already moving.

In a dozen long, raking strides, his horse had covered half the distance to the outlaw when Devlin tossed the rifle to one side, grabbed reins and horn and clawed his way on to the saddle. Beneath him, Verity's horse was wild-eyed, snorting through flared nostrils, ears flattened. As Devlin hauled on the reins and the bit jerked, its lips peeled back and with another shrill squeal, it leaped stiff-legged, came down with a jolt that clicked Devlin's teeth and spun about.

Standing too close, Verity was caught by a muscular shoulder, lifted and tossed aside like a dry leaf before the wind. She went down hard, arms instinctively flung up to shield her head from the flashing hooves. Then the horse had bounded over her. McGill was close, bearing down on the outlaw. With another burst of wild laughter, Devlin took the bronc straight across the trail and tore down a long slope

187

through the trees with a crackle of branches. As the sounds of his getaway faded, McGill flung himself from the saddle and dropped alongside his wife.

She was breathing hard, but as he took hold of her shoulder and she rolled and sat up, sweat-damp face streaked with dust, her eyes flashed fire.

'Oh, Ewan, Ewan!' she said, and he was amazed at the taut anger in her voice and at once realized that Diamond K was suddenly of enormous importance to her. 'Why, oh why, didn't you leave me, go after him and hold him here?'

'The further he is away, the better for all of us,' he said, and again was stunned by the stubborn reaction, the fierce shake of her head.

'No. Now he's gone we're a horse short, and when he overtakes Jack and that other killer they'll know for sure we're on their tail.' She was close to tears, a little girl sitting in the dust as Gord Brady rode to join them.

'Don't you see?' she said, clutching

McGill's hand, shaking it in her frustration, looking from him to the deputy. 'Now they *know*, they'll spare no effort. They'll ride like hell for Hancock — and with one of our horses carrying double, we stand no chance of catching them!'

16

There was a growing urgency in their manner, but there were fifty miles left to be covered, the light was fading with each mile and with it the heat. Crimson streaks painted the western horizon with dazzling strokes, the embers of a fire which, with sadness, they watched fade and die. With the sun gone, cloud cover appeared, stretching from horizon to horizon, dense enough to hide the moon and its candescent light. And with the cloud there came a sense of isolation. Two weary horses pounded onwards carrying Ewan McGill, Verity and Gord Brady ever deeper into the Singing Hills, but so strong was the sense of separateness that for mile after mile the riders exchanged not a single word.

Impossibly slowly, the fifty miles became twenty-five; as their impatience neared breaking point that twenty-five became twenty and continued to shrink as, miles back, the tail of the unseen dust-plume kicked up unendingly in their wake slowly drifted and settled. They caught the ripe stink of a dead steer, bore down upon it in a rush and a swift examination of the branded hide confirmed what Gord Brady had already surmised: they were crossing Diamond K land. And when the high rims of the ridges and hog-backs that formed the hollow in which the ranch was located became discernible — yet in so doing intensified the blackness below — Brady broke the silence.

'Riders,' he said, and coughed with something akin to embarrassment for his own words had broken like an intrusion.

'I hear them — I think.'

Against McGill's warm chest, encircled by his arms, Verity stirred, rousing herself from an uncomfortable doze.

'What?'

'Hush,' McGill said. 'Listen.'

The rumble was no stronger than the whisper of blood heard pulsing in the ears, the faintest roll of thunder heard from an impossible distance. Across the undulating land it waxed and waned — if any sound at all existed outside their dreams or imagination. Brady reined in his horse. McGill drew alongside, pulled up. They seemed to stop breathing, and McGill reached down to his restless horse's muzzle, soothed it by covering the moist warmth with his palm.

For a short while, they became a part of the night.

Then Brady let his breath go in an explosive snort of disgust.

'I was wrong.'

'Then two of us were,' said McGill.

'Does it matter?' Verity yawned, eased herself stiffly in the saddle. 'Diamond K's a working ranch. Riders'll come and go.'

'At this time? After a night on the town, riders try to stay in the saddle, not ride like the wind.'

'You were wrong — yet you heard that much?'

Brady shrugged in the darkness. 'If I heard anything,' he said, 'it wasn't a bunch of cowboys with their bellies full of liquor,' and McGill laughed softly.

'If,' Verity said. 'But all this talk's wasting time. From my aching bones I know we've been pushing hard for hours, but my recollections tell me it's still some miles to Fort Hancock. Instead of listening to the wind, we should keep moving.'

'The strength of a woman,' McGill said, and his arms squeezed her tight. 'I thought news of Johnny would break you . . . '

'Not now, not ever if I can help it — but get me to Hancock, Ewan, and with Diamond K ours we'll see if we can give that boy we loved some brothers he'd be proud of.'

And so they rode on, Brady still fretting over the riders he had heard, Verity nestled in the arms of Ewan

McGill in whose mind she had planted ideas that, for the first time, had dispelled some of his grief and shown him the way forward and how the new could be moulded from the old.

This time, as they rode, the silence was not of solitude but of expectancy for what lay ahead. It had been put there by the woman who had been bold enough to speak for them all; she was the weakest, yet the strongest; she led simply by being there.

They came down out of the hills when dawn was still hours away, rode swiftly between the buildings' false fronts where the oil lights of Fort Hancock swayed and creaked to the night breeze. But, as they rode deeper into town, it was clear that all was not well. At the end of the street, the lights were brighter. Men could be seen clustered outside a doorway through which light flooded the rutted dust. In that light, broken glass glittered.

'Gunsmoke,' McGill said, sniffing the air.

'They've been and gone,' Brady said. 'Those riders we heard — '

'Wait and see,' Verity said. 'It'll help if you know who in Hancock's wearing the badge these days.'

'Dave Neale. With my brother a lawyer it'd be strange if I didn't,' he said, but he was talking for the sake of it and in his voice there was a firm foreboding.

Heads had turned. It was noticeable that hands moved towards hips, and in at least one instance they saw the glint of steel as a pistol was half drawn.

Then a hard voice issued an order and, as the two ridden-down horses jingled up to the hitch rail outside the marshal's office and swayed to a halt, a stooped and angular man with a battered tin badge and a drooping moustache stepped away from the men gathered near the light.

'Gord?' he said, more softly. 'Back in town so soon — and ain't that a badge I see 'neath that vest?'

'Stranger things have happened,'

Brady said. 'What's goin' on here, Dave?'

'There ain't no easy way to tell it.' The marshal turned his head to spit in the dust, said, 'Three galoots rode up, bust into your brother's office when he was lockin' up, for some goddamn reason plugged him full of holes.'

Brady's face was tight. 'Dead?'

'Over at the doc's.' He shrugged helplessly. 'Hell, you know Mike. He was talkin' when Lynch started probin', and from the wink the old boy tossed me I reckon your brother'll pull through.'

'When was this?'

'Two hours ago, maybe a mite longer.'

As Brady wearily stepped down and took the marshal to one side, McGill slid off his horse and eased Verity out of the saddle. She groaned in a lady-like way when her feet touched the ground, smiled weakly as she straightened and clung to his arm.

'So Brady was right. Riding like the

wind, he said. We must have passed within half a mile of those devils.'

'Seems like it. But before they plugged his brother, did they get what they were after?'

'That's shutting the barn door when the cow's walked, Ewan. Jack was desperate for those deeds, but he won't bother with paperwork if he's on the premises. We couldn't stop him, so now it seems like we're too late. But I'll be damned if I rode all this way to lose . . . '

He took her arm, helped her on to the plankwalk and moved into the yellow light. Most of the men had drifted away. Brady was talking to the rawboned marshal and, as they drew near, McGill heard him say, 'Holdin' back in the Gulch helped get a young boy shot down in the street and — '

He broke off, looked quickly at Verity and spread his hands apologetically.

'It's all right,' she said. 'That's in the past, what matters is now.'

'My point exactly,' Brady said. 'We

know where those owlhoots have gone, so we should go get them, only — '

'Ma'am,' Dave Neale said dolefully, 'I'd raise a posse, but there's some reluctance on the part of certain lily-livered Hancock characters to risk their necks stormin' that place — '

'But I played on Diamond K as a child,' she cut in. 'Storming isn't necessary.'

McGill's grip on her arm tightened. 'You know a way in?'

'Does a child know the way into an orchard?'

'In the dark?'

'Blindfolded,' she said, and grinned.

'Three of 'em,' Dave Neale said gruffly, his eyes remembering. 'Bad as I've seen. Ma'am, it don't set easy with me, you bein' involved.'

'I'll look after her,' McGill said.

'Then that just leaves me Diamond K's owner to worry over.'

The words fell like stones in a pool, sank in a deepening silence.

'My pa died,' Verity said shakily, 'so

you can only be talking about Jack, who is the new owner but by force of arms — and why should his safety be of any concern?'

'No, ma'am,' Neale said, and again his voice was apologetic. 'Earl J's wife turned up — I guess that's your ma. She settled things with Mike Brady two days ago, and early this morning she moved on to the spread.'

17

A boy murdered, a woman reborn.

On the ride from Fort Hancock to the Diamond K, it was difficult for Ewan McGill to imagine his wife's torment. They rode off the trail and attacked the long slopes in the cold light of an approaching dawn, that time of day when men's spirits are at their lowest ebb, bodies at their most fragile, and a surprise assault will always bring an advantage. But the time before the battle is nerve-racking for those calling the tune, and for the woman who rode with them — led the way, because only she could slip them unseen into the natural stronghold — the advantages of her position, and the immense rewards success would bring, were withered to insignificance by the news given to her by Marshal Dave Neale.

The news was exhilarating, and

breathtaking in its unexpectedness, but the sheer, bubbling joy that had brought tears to her eyes had at once been quelled by the realization that yet another of her kin was in terrible danger; might perhaps, even as the marshal spoke, be lying dead on the floor of the ranch house to which she had so recently returned.

Verity McGill had handled those terrible thoughts with stoicism as they rode out of Hancock, any cries of horror or dismay that might have been shrieking for release held back by lips that were clamped firmly shut. And on that ride, with an understanding that had come without his bidding — the new being moulded from the old? — McGill left her to her thoughts.

Gord Brady had also been profoundly moved. It was, after all, his sister who had come back from the dead. The big man had taken the news with considerable aplomb, his eyes more concerned with the effect it might have on his niece. When it had been clear that she could handle it, and handle it well, he had to a certain extent withdrawn with his thoughts and the ride, though lively, was not notable for the conversation.

Fresh horses from Fort Hancock's livery barn — tough, ex-army broncs — carried them onwards at a fast lick. For most of the ride Verity was sheltered by the three men, for her turn to point the way would come. She rode with horses to either side and one, that of Gord Brady the experienced Diamond K ramrod, out front. If she had been in need she could have reached out to touch Marshal Dave Neale, or her husband. But as the skies lightened, imperceptibly, that lightness was reflected in her eyes and in her mood.

'Where we're heading, I used to pick flowers in the summer sun,' she said once, and laughed for the first time. 'Now we're about to ride through that notch to face armed men.'

'With no help,' Brady said. 'Your pa

died, every damn hand quit, walked off the spread.'

'When it brings us out, can we be seen from the house?'

'For all I know,' she told McGill, 'in twelve long years Pa might've knocked the house down and built it someplace else.'

'It's where it always was,' Gord Brady said. 'And anyhow, I think the notch you're talking about — if it's the same one I know — comes out behind the big barn. But your brother lived there, too: won't he be one step ahead of you?'

'Jack?' She grinned crookedly. 'Oh, no, Jack rode out before sun-up one fine morning, all set to tackle the big bad world with a rusty old Dragoon pistol.'

It was then, with tears once more bright in her eyes, that she spurred ahead.

They followed her in single file as the old deer trail twisted up through the trees towards where bald hills poked their heads at the sky. A glance ahead would have suggested it went all the way to a hog-back beyond which lay the Diamond K buildings, but after half a mile they became aware of a fault, a fissure in the hillside, and it was towards this that Verity led them at a gallop.

It was not a wash, nor an arroyo, but a wide crack caused by massive tremors that, countless centuries ago, had split the mountainside and moved onwards to be smothered by the vastness of the plains. The disturbance had been so far in the past that the scars were hidden beneath lush vegetation that clung to the raw cliff faces, gnarled and stunted trees that hung like native sentinels from the narrow ledges, moss and lichen that carpeted the rock floor of the fissure and dulled the sound of the horses' hoofs.

In that hour before dawn, entering the narrow passageway was like walking into the echoing caverns behind the deluge of a silent waterfall. The chill was damp and breathtaking, the light in those depths washed of all colour. To McGill it was a fearsome place.

The four riders had ridden a long way up to the notch and, as soon as they entered, the rock floor began to slope gently downwards. McGill knew Diamond K lay in a high, commanding hollow. Tucked in behind Verity, he could already see brighter light ahead. He twisted in the saddle to look back at Brady, saw the deputy nod his head in acknowledgement; saw Dave Neale grim faced at the rear.

Then, soon enough to set their nerves jangling, the fissure widened into a kind of roofless amphitheatre where now the horses' hooves rang on slabs of bare stone and, as they approached a lip masked by trees beyond which they could see the long slopes leading out of the Singing Hills and, beyond that again, the dazzle of the sun rising over the Texas plains, Verity held up her hand.

They encircled her, cursing softly as

hooves clattered and horses snorted their unease.

'It's not far down,' she said. 'A gentle slope through trees, the barn's back wall almost up against them.'

McGill had ridden forward. From close to the lip but under cover of the trees, he could see what lay below yet was still high enough to see over the barn to the log house, the long bunkhouse, the yard and broad corral.

'They're watchin' the wrong way,' he said and, as Brady joined him, he pointed across the corral to the figure sitting against a post where the trail wound down to the defile that was the only way in and out of Diamond K. A rifle gleamed in the early light, but the man's Stetson was tilted over his face.

'The right way, for us,' Brady said, 'and that's Blade Devlin, sleepin' on the job.'

'But if there's only one man out there,' Dave Neale said, 'the others are inside with the woman. That makes it tough.'

The look on Skinner's face changed to one of contempt. He had Brady down, McGill unarmed. As far as he was concerned, the battle was won.

McGill had other ideas.

The incident had taken no more than two seconds. Mrs Ketchum was frozen on the gallery. Devlin was running hard, but still had more than half the yard to cross. As Skinner turned his back and began to walk towards the drooping Gulch deputy, McGill broke into a run.

He cut behind Skinner. The lean owlhoot glanced his way, dismissed him as of no consequence. Ahead of McGill, Blade Devlin's eyes were fixed on the woman. In his mind she was the answer to all their problems. At that moment, nothing else mattered. Now nearing the house, he was unaware of McGill closing rapidly, face set, eyes blazing, hot blood from his ripped right hand leaving a red trail in the dust.

When realization dawned, it was too late.

McGill hit him like a train as the owlhoot at last caught sight of him, his mouth dropping open with shock. They went down in a boiling cloud of dust under the gallery's rail, snarling like mad dogs. As they rolled, first one man was on top, then the other. At the last moment, Skinner had brought the Winchester across his chest. It was between them, a steel barrier preventing McGill from getting close.

But that very barrier gave him his opportunity. One final roll left him on top, kneeling astride the owlhoot, held back by the Winchester gripped in Skinner's two fists. He had room to move. With a fierce yell of joy, McGill swung a wide looping right hook that started behind his hip and took the owlhoot on the side of the jaw. The yell of joy turned to a groan of pain as the damaged fist connected. The crack was like that of a log splitting. Devlin flopped back, blood from McGill's fist spraying across his face.

His eyes rolled, showing nothing but

the whites. He was out cold.

As he went limp between McGill's knees, across the yard a pistol cracked. On the gallery above, the woman choked off a scream. McGill came to his feet, swaying. A terrible feeling of dread swept over him, for himself, for the woman, for Gord Brady on his knees facing Clete Skinner — for Verity.

Then relief swept over him.

Skinner was down, a black shape stretched out in the dust of the yard.

Big, bearded Gord Brady was walking towards the house, his pistol smoking.

And then Verity was running past him, legs and arms pumping, face alight. She went straight past McGill and clattered up the gallery steps, and with a cry that was raw emotion she was in her mother's arms.

It was over.

★   ★   ★

217

'I took that Spencer off her and threw it as far as I could into the scrub,' Gord Brady said. 'She went lookin' for it — but then everything happened too damn fast.'

'I was wrong,' McGill admitted. 'If she'd murdered Skinner, neither of us could have lived with the memory.'

'In the end, that was my job.'

'I thought you were a gonner.'

'Got my big silver belt buckle to thank. The slug winded me, but . . . '

He shrugged, and McGill touched his shoulder, moved away.

They were in the yard. Verity and her mother had gone into the house. Already flies were droning as the rising heat of the day warmed the blood drying on three bodies.

'Every damn one of them was after it,' McGill said. 'In the end, they all lost.' He looked at Brady. 'I guess Verity's ma will want us to stay on and help her run the spread. She'll also need a foreman, and you bein' her brother . . . '

'I never did think on this as long-term employment,' Brady said, touching the tin badge on his vest. 'Fact is, it almost ended right here, in the way many such jobs do.'

'So . . . ?'

'So I'll sort this mess out, go talk to the people in Hancock, on the way back see if Jake Harding's still at Jackson's Hole, then report to Ed Thorpe in the Gulch. That should take no more than a couple of days.'

'You want to give your sister the good news?'

'It'll wait. She's been gone a long time. Getting to know Verity again is enough, for now.'

'Well,' McGill said, grinning, 'there'll be plenty to do when you get back.'

He shook Brady's hand, watched him begin the walk across the yard to the downed marshal of Hancock to begin the job of cleaning up, then turned and with a light heart ran up the steps to Verity and her mother.

We do hope that you have enjoyed reading this large print book.

Did you know that all of our titles are available for purchase?

We publish a wide range of high quality large print books including:
Romances, Mysteries, Classics
General Fiction
Non Fiction and Westerns

Special interest titles available in large print are:
The Little Oxford Dictionary
Music Book, Song Book
Hymn Book, Service Book

Also available from us courtesy of Oxford University Press:
Young Readers' Dictionary
(large print edition)
Young Readers' Thesaurus
(large print edition)

For further information or a free brochure, please contact us at:
Ulverscroft Large Print Books Ltd.,
The Green, Bradgate Road, Anstey,
Leicester, LE7 7FU, England.
Tel: (00 44) **0116 236 4325**
Fax: (00 44) **0116 234 0205**

Other titles in the
Linford Western Library:

STONE MOUNTAIN

Concho Bradley

The stage robbery had been accomplished by an old woman. Twine Fourch had never heard of a female being a highway robber before. He followed the trail all the way to a dilapidated log cabin up Stone Mountain. What happened after that no one could believe even after townsmen from Jefferson found the old log house and the skeletal dying old woman. But before the mystery could be solved there would be two unnecessary killings, a bizarre suicide and a lynching.

GUNS OF THE GAMBLER

M. Duggan

Destitute gambler Ben Crow arrives in Mallory keen to claim his inheritance, only to discover that rancher Edward Bacon has other ideas. Set up by Miss Dorothy, who had fooled him completely, Ben finds himself dangling on the end of a rope. Saved from death, Ben sets off in pursuit of Miss Dorothy, determined upon retribution. However, his quest for vengeance turns into a rescue mission when she is kidnapped by a crazy man-burning bandit.

SIDEWINDER

John Dyson

All Flynn wants is to be Marshal of Tucson, but he is framed by the territory's richest rancher, Frank Buchanan, and thrown into Yuma prison. Five years later Flynn comes out, intent on clearing his name and burning for vengeance. Fists thud, knives flash and bullets fly as he rides both sides of the law and participates in kidnapping and double-dealing. He is once again arrested for a murder of which he is innocent. Can he escape the noose a second time?

THE BLOODING OF JETHRO

Frank Fields

When Jethro Smith's family is murdered by outlaws, vengeance is the one thing on his mind. He meets the brother of one of the murderers, who attempts to exploit Jethro's grudge in the pursuit of his own vendetta. The local preacher, formerly a sheriff, teaches Jethro how to use a gun. With his new-found skills, Jethro and his somewhat unwelcome friend pit themselves against seemingly impossible odds. Whatever the outcome lead would surely fly.

SEVEN HELLS AND A SIXGUN

Jack Greer

Jim Cayman had been warned about Daphne Rankin, his boss's wife, and her little ways. When Daphne made a play for Jim and he resisted, the result was painful and about what he had feared. But suddenly matters went beyond the expected and he found himself left to die an awful death. Only then did he realise that there was far more than a woman scorned. He vowed that if he could escape from the hell-hole he would surely solve the mystery — and settle some scores.

CRISIS IN CASTELLO COUNTY

D. A. Horncastle

The first thing Texas Ranger Sergeant Brad Saunders finds when he responds to an urgent call for help from the local sheriff is the corpse of the public prosecutor floating in the Nueces River. Soon Brad finds himself caught in the midst of a power struggle between a gang of tough western outlaws and a bunch of Italian gangsters, whose thirst for bloody revenge knows no bounds. Brad was going to have all his work cut out to end the bloody warfare — and stay alive!